Home to Blue Stallion Ranch

STELLA BAGWELL

MILLS & BOON

First published in Great Britain 2019
by Mills & Boon, an imprint of HarperCollins*Publishers*
1 London Bridge Street, London, SE1 9GF

Large Print edition 2019

© 2019 Stella Bagwell

ISBN: 978-0-263-08351-4

MIX
Paper from
responsible sources
FSC **FSC® C007454**

This book is produced from independently certified FSC™ paper to ensure responsible forest management. For more information visit www.harpercollins.co.uk/green.

Printed and bound in Great Britain
by CPI Group (UK) Ltd, Croydon, CR0 4YY

After writing more than eighty books for Mills & Boon, **Stella Bagwell** still finds it exciting to create new stories and bring her characters to life. She loves all things Western and has been married to her own real cowboy for forty-four years. Living on the south Texas coast, she also enjoys being outdoors and helping her husband care for the horses, cats and dog that call their small ranch home. The couple has one son, who teaches high school mathematics and is also an athletic director. Stella loves hearing from readers. They can contact her at stellabagwell@gmail.com.

To all my horses, for the love
and happiness they've given me

Chapter One

Who the hell is that?

Holt Hollister pushed back the brim of his black cowboy hat and squinted at the feminine shape framed by the open barn door. He didn't have the time or energy to deal with a woman this morning. Especially one who was pouting because he'd forgotten to call or send flowers.

Damn it!

Jerking off his gloves, he jammed them into the back pocket of his jeans and strode toward the shapely figure shaded by the overhang. Behind him the loud whinny of a randy stallion drowned out the sounds of nearby voices, rattling feed buckets, the whir of fans, and the muffled music from a radio.

As soon as the woman spotted his approach, she stepped forward and into a beam of sunlight slanting down from a skylight. The sight very nearly caused Holt to stumble. This wasn't one of his girlfriends. This woman looked like she'd just stepped off an exotic beach and exchanged a bikini for some cowboy duds.

Petite, with white-blond hair that hung past her shoulders, she was dressed in a white shirt and tight blue jeans stuffed into a pair of black cowboy boots inlaid with turquoise and red thunderbirds. Everything about her said she didn't belong in his horse barn.

Frustration eating at him, he forced himself to march onward until the distance between them narrowed down to a mere arm's length and she was standing directly in front of him.

"Hello," she greeted. "Do you work here?"

Holt might forget where he'd placed his truck keys or whether he'd eaten in the past ten hours, but he didn't forget a woman. And he was quite certain he'd never laid eyes on this one before today. Even without a drop of makeup on her face, she was incredibly beautiful, with smooth, flawless skin, soft pink lips, and eyes that reminded him of blue velvet.

"It's the only place I've ever worked," he answered. "Are you looking for someone in particular?"

She flashed him a smile and at any other time or place, Holt would've been totally charmed. But not this morning. He'd spent a hellish night in the foaling barn and now another day had started without a chance for him to draw a good breath.

She said, "I am. I'm here to see Mr. Hollister. I was told by one of the ranch hands that I'd find him in this barn."

She was looking straight at him and for a brief second Holt was thrown off-kilter by her gaze. Not only direct, it was as cool as a mountain stream.

"Three Mr. Hollisters live on this ranch," he said bluntly. "You have a first name?"

"Holt. Mr. Holt Hollister."

He blew out a heavy breath. He might've guessed this greenhorn would be looking for him. Being the manager of the horse division of Three Rivers Ranch, he was often approached by horse-crazy women, who wanted permission to walk through the barn and pet the animals, as if he kept them around for entertainment.

"You're talking to him."

Those blue, blue eyes suddenly narrowed skeptically, as though she'd already decided he was nothing more than a stable hand. And he supposed he couldn't blame her. He'd not had time to shave this morning. Hell, he'd not even gone to bed at all last night. Added to that, the legs of his jeans were stained with afterbirth and smears of blood had dried to brown patches on his denim shirt.

"Oh. I'm Isabelle Townsend. Nice to meet you, Mr. Holt Hollister."

She extended her hand out to him and Holt wiped his palm against the hip of his jean before he wrapped it around hers.

"Is there something I can do for you, Ms. Townsend?" he asked, while wondering how such a soft little thing could have a grip like a vice.

She eased her hand from his. "I've been told you have nice breeding stock for sale. I'm looking to buy."

If Holt hadn't been so tired, he would've burst out laughing. She ought to be home painting her fingernails, or whatever it was that women like her did to amuse themselves, he thought. "Are you talking about cattle or horses? Or maybe you're looking for goats? If you are, I know a guy who has some beauties."

"Horses," she said flatly, while peering past his shoulder at the rows of stalls lining both sides of the barn. "This is a horse barn, isn't it? Or are you in the goat business now?"

The sarcasm in her voice was the same tone he'd used on her. And though he deserved it, her response irked him. Usually pretty women smiled at him. This one was sneering.

"I'm in the business of horses. And at this time, Three Rivers isn't interested in selling any. You should drive down to Phoenix and try the livestock auction. If you're careful with your bidding, you can purchase some fairly decent animals there. Now if you'll excuse me, I'm very busy."

Not waiting to hear her reply, he walked off and didn't stop until he was out the opposite end of the barn and out of Isabelle Townsend's sight.

* * *

Furious and humiliated, Isabelle turned on her heel and stalked out of the barn. So much for all she'd heard about Three Rivers Ranch and its warm hospitality. Apparently, those glowing recommendations didn't include Holt Hollister.

Outside in the bright Arizona sunlight, she crossed a piece of hard-packed ground to where her truck was parked next to a tall Joshua tree.

Jerking open the door, she was about to climb into the cab when a male voice called out to her.

Wondering if Holt Hollister had decided he'd behaved like an ass and had come to apologize, she turned to see it wasn't the arrogant horseman who'd followed her. This man was slightly taller and perhaps a bit older than Holt Hollister, but she could see a faint resemblance to the man she'd just crossed words with.

"Hello," he said. "I'm Blake Hollister, manager of the ranch."

He extended his hand in a friendly manner and Isabelle complied.

"I'm Isabelle Townsend," she introduced herself, then added dryly, "It's nice meeting you. I think."

His brows disappeared beneath the brim of his gray hat. "I happened to see you go in the horse barn five minutes ago. If you're looking for someone in particular, I might be able to help."

"I was looking for the man who manages your horse division. Instead I found a first-class jerk!" She practically blasted the words at him, then promptly hated herself for the outburst. This man couldn't be held responsible for his relative's boorish behavior. "Excuse me. I didn't mean to sound so cross."

"Isabelle Townsend," he thoughtfully repeated, then snapped his fingers. "You must be our new neighbor who purchased the old Landry Ranch."

Since she'd only moved here six weeks ago, she was surprised this man had heard of her. News in a small place must travel fast, she thought.

"That's right. I was interested in purchasing a few horses from Three Rivers. But unfortunately, your brother or cousin or whatever he is to you isn't interested in selling. Or showing a visitor good manners."

"I'm sorry about this, Ms. Townsend."

The ranch manager cast a rueful glance in the direction of the horse barn and Isabelle got the impression it wasn't the first time he'd had to apologize for his brother's behavior.

"Frankly, Mr. Hollister, I had heard this ranch was the epitome of hospitality. But after this morning, I have my doubts about that."

"Trust me. It won't happen again." His smile was apologetic. "You caught my brother at a bad time. You see, it's foaling season and he's working virtually 24/7 right now. I promise if you'll come back to the ranch tomorrow, I'll make sure Holt is on his best behavior."

Isabelle didn't give a damn about the horse manager. As far as she was concerned, the man could ride off into the sunset and never return.

"Honestly, Mr. Hollister, I have no desire to do business with your brother. Exhaustion isn't an excuse for bad manners."

"No. And I agree that Holt can be insensitive at times. But you'll find that when it comes to horses, he's the best."

He might be the best, but would dealing with the man be worth it? If it would help make her dream come true, she could surely put up with Mr. Arrogant for a few minutes, she decided.

Shrugging, she said, "All right, Mr. Hollister. I'll be back tomorrow."

He helped her into the truck, then shut the truck door and stepped back. And as Isabelle drove away, she wondered why she'd agreed to meet the good-looking horseman with a tart tongue for a second time. Solely for the chance to buy a few mares? Or did she simply want the pleasure of giving him a piece of her mind?

The answer to that was probably a toss-up, she decided.

"Holt? Are you in there?"

The sound of Blake's loud voice booming through the open doorway penetrated Holt's sleep-addled brain. Groggily, he lifted his head just in time to see his older brother step into the messy room he called his office.

"I'm right here. What's the matter? Is Cocoa having trouble?" He leaned back in the desk chair and wiped a hand over his face.

"As far as I know, nothing is wrong with Cocoa. I saw her five minutes ago. She was standing and the baby was nursing."

"Thank God. I had to call Chandler back to the ranch to deal with her afterbirth. I was afraid she might be having complications," he explained, then squinted a look at Blake's dour expression. "What's the matter with you? You look like you've been eating green persimmons."

"That task would probably be easier than trying to fix your mess-ups," Blake retorted.

This wiped the cobwebs from Holt's brain. "My mess-ups? What are you talking about?"

Blake shoved a stack of papers to one side and eased a hip onto the corner of the desk. "Don't feign ignorance. You know damned good and well I'm talking about Isabelle Townsend. The blonde who left the horse barn with smoke pouring out of her ears. What the hell did you say to her anyway?"

Holt used both hands to scrub his face again. "Not much. I basically made it clear that I didn't have time for her. Which is hardly a lie. You know that."

Blake blew out a heavy breath. "Yes, I know it. But in this case, you should've made time. Or, at the very least, been polite to the woman."

Holt picked up a coffee cup and peered at the cold black liquid inside. He'd poured the drink about five hours earlier, but never found a chance to drink it. Now particles of dust were floating over the surface. "What is the big deal, Blake? It was very clear to me that the woman had no legitimate business here on the ranch. I seriously doubt she's ever straddled a horse in her entire life. We'll probably never see her again."

"Wrong. I invited her to return tomorrow. And I made a personal promise to her that you'd be behaving like a human being instead of a jackass."

Holt plunked the coffee cup back to the desktop. "Oh, hell, Blake, you have no idea how I behaved with Isabelle what's-her-name. You weren't there."

"I didn't have to be. I know how you are whenever you run out of patience. Like I said, a jackass."

"Okay, okay. I wasn't nice. I'll admit it. But I'm running on empty. And just looking at her rubbed me the wrong way."

Blake arched a brow at him. "Really? She was damned pretty. Since when has a pretty woman got your dander up? Unless—" His eyes narrowed with suspicion. "Dear Lord, I hope you didn't make a pass at her. Is that what really happened?"

"No! Not even close!" Holt rose from the chair and began to move restlessly around the jumbled room.

His mother often mentioned that he needed a nicer office, one that was fitting for a respected horse trainer, but Holt always balked at the idea. He liked the dust and the jumble. He liked having metal filing cabinets filled with papers instead of flash drives and computers with spreadsheets. If he wanted to throw a dirty saddle across the back of a chair, he did. If he wanted to toss a pile of headstalls and bridles into a corner of the room, he didn't worry about how it looked or smelled. He was in the business of horses. Not ostentatious surroundings. Or technical gadgets.

"Yeah, pretty women and I go hand in hand," he went on with a dose of sarcasm. "Except I don't like it when they pretend to be something they aren't."

"I don't get you, Holt. You don't know Isabelle Townsend. Why you've made this snap decision about her, I'll never understand. But I'm telling you, you've got it all wrong. She's purchased the old Landry Ranch and has intentions of turning it into a horse farm. And from what I hear about the woman, she has enough riding trophies to fill up this room."

Holt stopped in his tracks and stared at his brother. "Who says?"

"Emily-Ann for one. And working at Conchita's, you know she hears everything."

Holt sputtered. "Sure, Blake. Working at a coffee shop means she hears gossip."

"This is more than gossip," Blake countered. "Emily-Ann has become fairly good friends with the woman."

Holt looked away from his brother and down at the dusty planked floor. This part of the foaling barn had been built many years before Holt was born and the cypress boards, though durable, were a fire hazard. The floor actually needed to be ripped out and replaced with concrete, but like many parts of the century-and-a-half-old ranch, they remained as pieces of tradition.

"The old Landry Ranch, you say? That means she's our neighbor on the north boundary."

"Right," Blake replied. "And we don't need any kind of friction with a neighbor. So you think you can play nice in the morning?"

Holt grinned. "Sure. I'll be so sweet, she'll think she's covered in molasses."

Blake rolled his eyes. "I don't think you need to spread it on that thick, brother.

Just be yourself. No. On second thought, that could be dangerous. Just be congenial."

Holt's weary chuckle was more like a groan. "Don't worry, Blake. I'll be on my best behavior."

By the time Isabelle reached the outskirts of Wickenburg, she'd managed to push her simmering frustration aside and set her thoughts on the breakfast she'd missed earlier this morning. Endless chores were waiting for her back at the ranch, and it would make more sense to go home and fix herself a plate of eggs and toast. But she was already close to town, and after that humiliating encounter with Holt Hollister, taking time for coffee and a pastry at Conchita's would be a treat she desperately needed.

After driving through the main part of Wickenburg, she turned onto a sleepy side street where the tiny coffee shop was located. Shaded by two old mesquite trees, the building's slab pine siding was weathered to a drab gray. Worn stepping stones led up to a small porch with a short overhang.

At the moment, the single wooden door stood open to the warm morning and Isabelle could hear the muted sounds of music. As she stepped inside the dim interior, she was met with the mouthwatering scents of fresh baked pastries and brewing coffee.

An elderly man with a cane was at the counter. Isabelle stood to one side and waited patiently while Emily-Ann sacked his order.

"Hi, Isabelle!" the waitress greeted. "I'll be right back as soon as I help Mr. Perez out with his things."

"Sure. Take your time. I'm in no hurry," Isabelle assured her.

The gentleman waved a dismissive hand at the young, auburn-haired woman and spoke something to her in rapid Spanish. Emily-Ann replied in the same language and made a shooing gesture toward the door.

"He insists he can carry his order out to the car on his own," she explained to Isabelle. "But I'm not going to let that happen."

While Emily-Ann assisted the customer, Isabelle stepped up to the glass cases holding a huge array of pastries and baked treats. She was still trying to decide between the brownies and the apple fritters when Emily-Ann returned and gave Isabelle a tight hug.

Laughing, Isabelle hugged her back. "You must have missed me!"

"I have!" Emily-Ann exclaimed, a wide smile lighting up her pretty freckled face. "You've not been in for a few days."

"I've been busy. So busy, in fact, that I missed breakfast this morning." Isabelle pointed to a top shelf. "Give me a brownie and an apple fritter. And a large regular coffee with cream."

Emily-Ann, who was the same age as Isabelle, looked at her in disbelief. "A brownie and an apple fritter? And you look like that? Do you know how frustrated that makes me? Just breathing the air in here makes me gain a pound!"

Isabelle shook her head. "You look lovely. I only wish I had your height. For the first fifteen years of my life, I was called shorty."

"That's better than being called freckles." Emily-Ann turned to a counter behind her and filled a cup with coffee. "Do you want this to go?"

"No. I don't want to gobble it down while I drive. I want to enjoy every bite."

"Great," she said. "The customers have let up for the moment so I'll join you. That is, if you'd like the company."

"C'mon. I'd love your company."

The two women walked outside and sat down at one of the small wrought iron tables and chairs sitting in the shade of the mesquites.

"So what's been going on with you since I was here?" Isabelle asked as she broke off a piece of the brownie and popped it into her mouth.

Emily-Ann tilted her head from side to side in a nonchalant expression. "Nothing new. At this time of year, lots of snowbirds come in for coffee. Most of them are friendly and want to chat and ask questions about things to see and do around here. Honestly, Isabelle, when you've lived in one little town all your life, you don't really see things as a tourist. For example, that saguaro over there across the street. The tourists ooh and aah over it. To me, it's just a saguaro."

"That's because you see it every day." Isabelle sipped her coffee, hoping the caffeine would revive her from the long morning she started before daylight. "But think of it this way, one of those snowbirds that walk into the coffee shop might be your Mr. Right."

Emily-Ann grimaced. "I'm not sure I want to look for a Mr. Right anymore. The men I've dated have all turned out to be stinkers."

Isabelle shrugged. "At least you weren't like me and made the mistake of marrying the wrong man."

"From what you've told me, your ex would've been happy to stay married. And you did say that the two of you are still friends. Are you sure you don't regret getting a divorce?"

"Trevor was a good guy. A nice guy. But he—" He just hadn't loved her. Not with the deep, abiding love that Isabelle had craved. "Well, he was a great companion. Just not a husband."

Shaking her head, Emily-Ann sighed. "I'm not sure I get that. But as long as you think you're better off now, then that's all that really matters, I suppose."

Isabelle finished the brownie and unwrapped the square of wax paper from the fritter. "I am better off. I'm following my dreams."

Emily-Ann leaned back in her chair. "How is the ranch coming along? Have you found any horses to buy?"

Instead of blurting the curse word burning the tip of her tongue, Isabelle snorted. "Actually, I drove out to Three Rivers this morning to look at their horses, but I didn't get to first base."

"Oh, what happened? Out of all of the horses they have, surely you could find something that suited you."

"Ha! All I got to see was an arrogant cowboy and he promptly sent me on my way."

Emily-Ann's mouth fell open. "You mean Holt? *He* sent you packing?"

"He did. Emily-Ann, I thought you told me he was a charming guy and that he'd be easy to do business with. The guy is a first-class jerk!" Isabelle huffed out a breath and reached for her coffee.

Emily-Ann was perplexed. "I don't understand how that could've happened. But he's dreamy-looking. Right?"

Isabelle sipped the hot drink and tried not to think about the way Holt Hollister had looked standing there in front of her with his long legs parted and his arms folded against his broad chest. Dreamy? He'd looked rough around the edges and as tough as rawhide. "I'll admit he's sexy, but not the sort I dream about. I like manners and kindness in a man."

Emily-Ann batted a hand through the air. "Holt knows all about manners. Him sending you away—that's just not the man I know, and I've been friends with the whole family since I was a very little girl."

Isabelle shrugged, while trying not to take the man's behavior personally. "There must've been something about me that Holt didn't like. Or maybe something I said. Like hello," she added dryly. "No matter. Blake invited me to come back tomorrow and I'm going to take him up on the invitation."

Emily-Ann looked relieved. "Oh, so you met Blake. He's a real gentleman."

"I'll put it this way, he's nothing like his brother," Isabelle replied.

"So what did you think about Three Rivers? It's quite a place, isn't it?"

Nodding, Isabelle admitted, "Beautiful. But nothing like I was expecting. I thought the main ranch house would be a hacienda-type mansion surrounded by a stone wall with an elaborate gated entrance. Instead, it was a homey three-story house with wood siding and a front porch for sitting."

Emily-Ann sighed. "The Hollisters are a homey bunch. Guess that's why the family is so well liked. They're just regular folks. Even though they have oodles of money."

Isabelle's ex had also had oodles of money. Perhaps not as much as the Hollisters, but he'd had enough to give her a tidy fortune in the divorce settlement. Money was necessary, and Isabelle would be lying if she said she didn't appreciate the life it was allowing her to lead. Particularly with her plans to build a horse farm. But money wasn't everything. In the end, Trevor's money hadn't made up for his inability to love her.

"Well, if I don't meet a different Holt tomorrow, I'm going to suggest he drive up to the Grand Canyon and take a flying leap off the South Rim."

"Ouch. He must have really rubbed you the wrong way."

Just the thought of Holt Hollister rubbing her in any way sent a shiver down Isabelle's spine. Maybe the women around here went for the barbarian type, but she didn't.

Purposely focusing her attention on the apple fritter, Isabelle said, "Let's talk about something else, shall we? I don't want to ruin the rest of my day."

* * *

For the first night in the past ten nights, no foals were born and Holt managed to sleep until four thirty in the morning without being disturbed. Even so, the moment he opened his eyes, he jerked to a sitting position and stared around the bedroom, disoriented.

What was he doing in bed and what the heck had happened while he'd been asleep? Swinging his legs over the side of the mattress, he reached for the phone on the nightstand and punched the button for the direct line to the foaling barn. It rang six times before someone finally picked it up and by then Holt was wide-awake.

"Yep."

"Matt, is that you?" Matthew Waggoner was the ranch foreman and had been for several years. His job was mostly handling the cowhands, the cattle, and everything that entailed. He usually stayed away from the mares and foals.

"Yep, it's me. What's wrong?"

"Why are you in the foaling barn?" Holt asked. "Has something happened?"

"No. Everything is quiet. I'm spelling Leo. He's dead on his feet. Sounds like you are, too."

Holt raked a hand through his tumbled hair, then reached for the jeans he'd left lying on the floor by the bed. "When I woke up and realized I'd been in bed all night, it scared me."

Matthew chuckled. "That's a hell of a thing to be scared about. Hang up and go back to sleep. The mares in the paddock are all happy and the hands and I won't be leaving out of the ranch yard until six anyway."

"Thanks, Matt. But my sleep is over. I'll be down as soon as I grab something from the kitchen."

In the bathroom, he sluiced cold water onto his face, then ran a comb through his dark hair. The rusty brown whiskers on his face hadn't seen a razor in three days, but he wasn't going to bother shaving this morning. He had more important worries.

After he'd thrown a denim shirt over his jeans and tugged on a pair of worn cowboy boots, he hurried down to the kitchen, where Reeva was already shoving an iron skillet filled with buttermilk biscuits into the oven. The scents of frying bacon and chorizo filled the warm room.

"Got any tortillas warm yet, old woman?" Holt asked as he sneaked up behind the cook and pecked a kiss on her cheek.

Without batting an eye, she pointed to a platter stacked with breakfast tacos wrapped in aluminum foil. "The tacos are already made. What do you think I do around here anyway? Sit reading gossip magazines or lie in bed? Like you?"

In her early seventies, Reeva was a tall, thin woman with straight, iron gray hair that was usually pulled into a ponytail or braid. She'd been working as the Hollister cook since before Holt had been born and now after all these years, she was a part of the family. Which was all for the best, he thought, since the little family she'd once had were all moved away and out of her life.

"Ha! I've seen you lounging around in the den reading gossip magazines and drinking coffee," Holt teased as he snatched up three of the tacos.

Reeva swatted the spatula at his hand. "Get out of here, you worthless saddle tramp."

"Don't worry, I'm going. As soon as I find my insulated cup."

"Right behind you. On the cabinet. And don't go out without your jacket. It's cold this morning."

"It's a good thing you're around to tell me what to do, Reeva. Otherwise, I'd be in a hell of a mess." He grabbed up the stainless steel cup and headed toward the door that led to the backyard.

"You stay in a mess even with my help," she said tartly, then added, "I'll send Jazelle down with some pastries later. And don't call me old woman."

Holt looked over his shoulder and winked at her. "Reeva, you look as fresh as a spring rose."

Reeva continued to flip the frying bacon. "You wouldn't know what a spring rose looked like. But I love you anyway."

"Right back at ya, old woman."

At the door, he levered on a gray Stetson and, to please Reeva, pulled on a Sherpa-lined jacket. After stuffing the tacos into one of the pockets to keep them warm on the long walk to the foaling barn, he stepped outside and was promptly slammed in the face with a cold north wind.

Ducking his head, he left the backyard and started toward the massive ranch yard in the distance. Along the way, he passed the bunkhouse where most of the single ranch hands lived. The scents of coffee and frying sausage drifted out from the log building and Holt figured the guys would be sitting down to breakfast any minute now, which was served at five on most mornings. Once in a while, he and Blake would join the group for the early meal, just to share a few casual minutes with the hardworking employees. But the bunkhouse cook was a crusty old fellow, who couldn't begin to match Reeva's kitchen skills.

At the cattle pens, there were already a half dozen cowboys spreading feed and hay. Dust billowed from the stirring hooves, a sign that so far the winter had been extremely dry. Grass on the range was getting as scarce as hen's teeth and Matthew had already warned Blake that the hay Three Rivers had baled back in the spring would soon be gone. As for the Timothy/alfalfa mix Holt fed the horses, he'd already been forced to get tons of it shipped in from northern Nevada.

At times like these, Holt figured Blake acquired a few more gray hairs at his temples. As manager of the ranch, his brother carried a load on his shoulders and he worried. But Holt didn't worry. Not about the solvency of the ranch. After a hundred and seventy-one years, he figured the place would keep on standing strong. No, the only thing he worried about was keeping the horses healthy. And his mother.

For the most part, Holt could control the well-being of the Three Rivers' remuda, but his mother was a different matter. Lately she was doing a good job of acting like she was happy. But Holt and his siblings weren't fooled. She was keeping something from the family.

Chandler wanted to think she'd fallen in love and was trying to hide it, but Holt didn't go along with his brother's idea. A woman in love had a look about her that was impossible to hide and his mother didn't have it.

When Holt reached the horse barn, the hands were already feeding the few mares that were stalled with their new foals. T.J., the barn manager, met Holt in the middle of the wide alleyway.

"Mornin', Holt," he greeted. "Everything is quiet. No problem with Ginger. She seems to have taken to her little boy. He's been standing and nursing and already looks stronger than he did two hours ago."

Holt wasn't surprised to hear T.J. had already been at the barn for two or three hours. He was a dedicated young man with an affinity for horses. He'd come to work for the ranch six years ago and since then had proved his worth over and over.

"That's happy news. I was afraid we might have to put him on a nurse mare." Grinning now, Holt patted his jacket pocket. "I have breakfast tacos. If you're hungry, I'll share."

"Thanks, Holt, but I promised William I'd eat at the bunkhouse this morning. Now that you're here, I'll mosey on over there."

"Better do more than mosey or there won't be anything left."

"Right. I'll be back in a few minutes." The barn manager turned on his heel and hurried out of the barn.

On the way to his office, Holt made a short detour to Ginger's stall. As T.J. had informed him, the colt was looking remarkably stronger since his birth yesterday. The fact that the first-time mare was now bonding with her baby was a huge relief and he smiled as he watched her lick the white star on the colt's forehead.

"He's a good-looking boy. Big boned, bright eyed and straight legs. By the time he's a weanling, he'll be strong and sturdy."

The unexpected female voice had him whirling around to see Isabelle Townsend had walked up behind him. The sight of her at any time of the day would've surprised him, but he doubted it was daylight yet. Blake had told him she'd probably return to the ranch today, but he'd not mentioned she might show up at five in the morning!

"Ms. Townsend," he said in the way of greeting. "You're out early."

To his surprise, she must've forgiven his nasty behavior yesterday. There wasn't anything sarcastic in the smile on her face. On the contrary. It was warm enough to chase away the chill in the barn.

"Yesterday you were too busy to deal with me. This morning I came early in hopes I'd catch you before that happened."

He had a thousand and one things to do, including eating the meager breakfast he was carrying in his pocket. He didn't have time for Isabelle Townsend. Not this morning, or any morning. But he'd promised Blake he'd be a gentleman and one thing Holt never wanted to do was break his word to his big brother.

"I was headed to my office. If you'd like to join me, we can talk there." He turned away from Ginger's stall. "Have you had breakfast?"

"No. But I'm fine. Sometimes I don't bother with that meal."

From the looks of her, she didn't bother with eating much at all. Yesterday he'd noticed she was petite. This morning, he could see she was even smaller than he remembered. Even with the heels of her cowboy boots adding to her height, he doubted the top of her head would reach the middle of his chest. The notion struck him that he could pick her up with one arm and never feel the strain.

But he had no plans to get that close to their pretty neighbor, Holt decided. Not unless she wanted him to.

Chapter Two

Walking to his office, Isabelle was careful to keep a respectable distance from Holt Hollister. She had no idea if Emily-Ann's remarks about him being a ladies' man were true or just rumors. Either way, she didn't want to give him the impression that she was interested in anything more than his horses.

"You must have assumed I start the day early," he said.

"All horse trainers start the day long before daylight," she replied. "That is, the good ones do."

He let out a dry chuckle. "Does that mean you put me in the company of the good ones?"

His voice was raspy, like he'd just lifted his head from the pillow after a long sleep. The sound shivered right through her.

"I've heard a lot about you, Mr. Hollister, but I don't go by hearsay. So I can't really answer your question—yet."

Her reply didn't appear to annoy him, rather he had an amused look on his face. "I've heard some things about you, too. But I don't rely on hearsay either."

Isabelle couldn't imagine what he might have heard about her. She doubted it could've been much, though. Since she'd moved here, she'd only made a few acquaintances around town.

At the end of the barn, he opened a door

on the left and motioned for her to pro-
ceed him through it.

Isabelle stepped past him and into the
small room that looked more like a tack
room than an office. Jammed with a
messy desk, two wooden chairs, and a
row of file cabinets, it was also littered
with bits and bridles, saddle blankets
and pads, leather cinches and breast har-
nesses. In one corner, there was even a
worn saddle thrown over a wooden saw-
horse.

"Have a seat," he invited. "You might
want to wipe the dust off first, though.
We don't do much cleaning out here in
the barn. It doesn't do much good."

"I'm used to dust." And mud. Rain and
snow. Heat and cold. Early and late. In the
horse business, a person had to get used
to all those things and much, much more.

While she settled herself in one of the
wooden chairs sitting in front of the desk,
he placed the stainless steel vacuum cup

he'd been carrying on the desktop, then walked over to a heater and adjusted the thermostat.

Back at the desk, he took a seat in a leather executive chair and picked up the receiver on a landline telephone. After punching a button, he promptly said, "Reeva, as soon as Jazelle shows up—oh, she has—that's good. Send her on with the pastries, would you? And more coffee." He paused. "That's right. The horse barn. Not the foaling barn. Thanks."

He hung up the phone, then leveled his attention directly on Isabelle. "My brother Blake tells me you've bought the old Landry ranch. Are you living there now?"

Isabelle nodded. "I am. The Landry family had been out of the house for a long time and it needed some repairs. Fortunately, I've gotten most of them done. At least to where the place is comfortable now. The barns and utility sheds were in far better shape than the house. There are still areas of the ranch that need plenty of work and changes made, but it's good enough for me to start adding horses to the ones I already have."

He looked somewhat surprised. "You already have horses?"

"That's right. Ten in all. Two geldings for work purposes and eight broodmares that are currently in foal to a stallion back in Albuquerque, New Mexico. I don't have a stallion of my own yet. But like I said yesterday, I'm looking to buy. Preferably a blue roan that's proven to throw color and produce hearty babies."

He suddenly grinned and Isabelle felt her breath catch in her throat. She could definitely see why the rumors of being a ladies' man followed him around. He was charming without even trying. But she'd been around men of his caliber before. They weren't meant to be taken seriously.

"We'd all like one of those, Ms. Townsend."

She shook her head. "Please call me Isabelle. After all, we're neighbors. Even if it is eighteen miles to my place."

"Okay, Isabelle. Since you seem determined to add to your workload, I'll show you a few mares I might be willing to part with. But I don't have a stallion I want to sell. Maybe in a year or two. But not now."

She shrugged one shoulder. "That's okay. I'll be happy to look at anything you have."

The room was getting nice and warm so Isabelle untied the fur-edged hood of her jacket and allowed it to slip to her back. As she shook her hair free, she noticed he was watching her as though he was trying to gauge what was beneath the surface. The idea was disturbing, but it didn't offend her. She was a complete stranger to the man. In his line of business, he had a right to wonder about her character and how she might care for the animals he sold her.

"You mentioned Albuquerque. Is that where you're from originally?"

She shook her head. "No. I was born in California and lived there all of my life until I, uh, married and moved with my husband to New Mexico."

Beneath the brim of his battered gray hat, she could see one of his dark brows quirk upward.

"Oh. You're married then?"

She felt like telling him that her marital status really had nothing to do with her buying horses. But she didn't want to irk him again. At least, not before she had a chance to do business with the man. Besides, her being a divorcée was hardly a secret, even if it was something that made her feel like a failure as a woman.

"No. I've been divorced for more than a year now. He still lives in New Mexico. I decided to move here." She gave him a wide smile to let him know she was feeling no regrets about her ex or the move to

Arizona. "And so far I love it. The Landry Ranch was just what I was looking for."

He reached in the pocket of his jacket and pulled out three long items wrapped in aluminum foil and placed them on the desk. From the scents drifting her way, Isabelle guessed he'd been carrying around his breakfast.

"I imagine you've changed the ranch's name by now," he said.

Her smile grew wider. "I have. To Blue Stallion Ranch. I might not own him now. But I will make my dream come true one day."

"I see. Sounds like you've put a lot of thought into this."

"When a woman dreams for her future, she does put a lot of thought into it. And the dream of Blue Stallion Ranch is something I've had for a long time."

He started to say something, but a knock on the open door of the office interrupted him. Isabelle looked over her shoulder to see a tall blond woman about her own age entering the room carrying a large lunch bucket and a tall metal thermos.

"Breakfast is here," she announced cheerfully. "The pastries are fresh and the coffee is hot, so you'd better dig in."

"Jazelle, you're an angel in blue jeans," he told the woman. "I'll dance at your wedding with cowbells on."

Jazelle pushed aside a stack of papers and placed the containers on the desktop. "Ha! You won't be wearing cowbells or anything else to my wedding. 'Cause that ain't going to happen. And yes, I said *ain't*—so there!"

He responded to the woman's caustic reply with a loud laugh. "Sure, Jazelle. You and Camille have sworn off men for the rest of your lives. I've heard it all before, but I don't believe a word of it."

She glared at him. "Well, you'd better believe it, buddy! And if you had any sense, you'd swear off women, too."

He coughed awkwardly and Jazelle turned an apologetic look on Isabelle.

"Sorry," she said, then shaking her head, she laughed. "Uh—Holt and I like to tease. We really love each other. Don't we, Holt?"

He grinned. "Just like brother and sister," he said, then gestured to Isabelle. "Jazelle, meet Isabelle. She's our new neighbor to the north. She's a horsewoman."

Isabelle rose and extended her hand to the other woman. "Nice to meet you, Jazelle. And thank you for bringing the breakfast. It smells heavenly."

Jazelle's handshake was hearty and sincere and Isabelle liked her immediately.

"The cook and I bake pastries every other day. These just came out of the oven." She continued to eye Isabelle. "I'm sorry I'm staring. But you're just too darn pretty to be a horsewoman."

Isabelle laughed. "And you're too kind."

Jazelle left the office and Isabelle looked around to see Holt had opened the lunch bucket and was in the process of filling two foam cups with coffee.

"Let's eat," he said. "There's creamer and sugar for your coffee if you want it. And take what pastries you want. I have three chorizo and egg tacos. You're welcome to one of them, too."

"No, thanks. One of these cinnamon rolls will be enough." She poured creamer into her coffee and with the cup and roll in hand, she sat back down in the chair.

Through the open doorway, Isabelle could hear the horses exchanging whinnies and the familiar clanking of gates as each stall door was opened and closed. Above those sounds was the faint hum of a radio and the noise of the workers as they called to each other.

Someday, she thought, her barn would sound like this. Look like this. With mares and foals everywhere and plenty of ranch hands taking care of the chores. As much as Trevor had tried to make her happy, he'd never shared Isabelle's dream of having a horse farm. He'd only tolerated her obsession with equines because he'd been smart enough to know if he'd given her an ultimatum, she would've chosen the horses over him.

"Is working with horses something you've done for a while?" he asked. "Or is this a new venture for you?"

Isabelle swallowed a bite of the roll before she answered. "I first started riding when I was five years old. That's when my mom introduced me to a little brown pony named Albert. And I fell in love. By the time I got to be a teenager, I wanted to be a jockey, but Mom steered me away from that and into reining and cutting competitions. She considered being a jockey too dangerous."

He grunted with amusement. "Walking through the mare's paddock at feeding time is dangerous."

"That's true. But anyway, I got into the reining thing in a big way and eventually started training for breeders in southern

California. After I moved to New Mexico, I began to acquire the mares."

"I see. So until now, you've not actually had a horse ranch?"

She sipped the coffee, then shook her head. "Believe it or not, my ex-husband was overly generous in the divorce settlement just so I'd have plenty to purchase the property and the horses."

The taco in his hand paused halfway to his mouth. "That's hard to fathom."

No. She didn't expect him to understand. Something about Holt Hollister said he was the sort who'd love with all his heart, or not at all. And whatever he possessed, he'd fight to keep. Whether that be a wife, or material assets.

"I realize it sounds a bit crazy," she said. "But we're still good friends. And he wants me to be happy. Add to that, the man has more money than he knows what to do with. That's the way with some folks in the oil industry. Money flows and things are acquired so easily that after a while everything loses its luster." She cleared her throat, confused and embarrassed that she'd shared such personal things with this man. "Anyway, Trevor is a good and generous man. And he's made it possible to invest in my dreams."

"Lucky you."

His quipped reply rankled her, but she carefully hid her reaction. "There was nothing lucky about it. I didn't ask for the money. Or the divorce."

His gaze dropped to the cup he was holding. "Sorry. I shouldn't have said that."

Was he really sorry? She doubted it. But then his opinion of her personal life hardly mattered. After today, she wouldn't be rubbing shoulders with the man.

"Forget it," she told him. "I have."

She might've already forgotten, but Holt hadn't. Damn it!

He didn't know how their conversation had turned to such personal issues. One

minute they'd been talking about her connection to horses and the next she was
telling him about her divorce.

Hell! He didn't care if she was married
with five kids or devotedly single. He
didn't care if she had a good and generous ex-husband. And he sure didn't care
that she was the sexiest woman he'd ever
laid eyes on. To Holt, she was horse buyer.
Nothing more. Nothing less.

"Has your family always owned Three
Rivers Ranch?"

Her question jerked Holt out of his rev-
erie and he looked at her as he swallowed
down the last bite of taco.

"The Hollisters first built this ranch
back in 1847. Since then it's always been
a family thing."

"Wow! That must go back through several generations," she said, then shrugged.
"I can't remember the house my parents
and I lived in when I entered middle
school, much less know what sort of place

they had when I was born. They were no-
mads. Still are."

"So you think you want to root down."
He wished she'd quit talking about homes
and family. She didn't look the sort and
he was as far from a family man as Earth
was from Mars.

"More than anything," she said with
conviction.

Jazelle had brought a few little pecan
tortes along with the cinnamon rolls. He
gobbled down two of them and was finishing his coffee as fast as he could when
she said, "I realize you're in a hurry to
get me out of your hair, but at the pace
you're eating, you're going to have stomach issues."

Dear Lord, was there nothing she
missed? "I always eat fast. Otherwise, I
might not have the chance to eat at all. If
you're finished with your coffee, we'll go
have a look at the horses."

Smiling faintly, she leaned forward and

gracefully placed her cup on the edge of his desk. "I'm ready any time you are."

Rising from the desk chair, he pulled on his jacket and buttoned it up to his throat. By then, she'd gotten to her feet and fastened the hood over all that white-blond hair and pulled on a pair of fuzzy black mittens. She looked as sweet as Christmas candy and as fragile as a sparrow's wing. How could this woman ever manage to work a horse ranch?

That's none of your concern, Holt. All you need to do is keep your mind on your job and off the way Isabelle Townsend looks or sounds or smells. She's not your type. She never will be.

Shoving away the mocking reminder in his head, he gestured toward the door. "You're welcome to look at the mares and babies here in the barn, but none of them are for sale. Anything I might be willing to part with is outside."

"I'd love to take a leisurely look. But

you're just as busy as I am. Let's just head on outside."

Her response should have pleased him. The quicker he could get this meeting over with, the better. Yet he had to admit a part of him had wanted to show her some of the fine babies his mares had delivered in the past few days. Like a proud dad, he would've enjoyed sticking out his chest and preening just a little. But she wasn't going to give him the chance.

"Fine," he said. "We'll exit the barn on this end."

Outside the building, she followed him over to a ten-acre patch surrounded by a tall board fence.

"This is where I keep the mares that have two or three weeks before foaling," he told her. "When they start getting to that point in their gestation, I like to keep a closer eye on them."

"Do you have a resident vet here on the ranch?"

"My older brother Chandler is the vet," he told her. "If something comes up that I can't handle, he'll come running."

"I'm just now putting two and two together," she said thoughtfully. "He must run the Hollister Animal Hospital. Does he live here on the ranch, too?"

Her question reminded Holt that he and his baby sister, Camille, were the only Hollister siblings left who didn't have a spouse and children. As for Camille, he couldn't speak for her wants and wishes, but on most days Holt was happy he was still footloose and fancy-free. There were too many women in the world to waste his life on just one.

"Yes, with his wife, Roslyn, and baby daughter, Evelyn."

A bright smile suddenly lit her face. "Oh, so there's a baby in the house. How nice."

"It's nice and noisy. There are three babies in the house. Blake has twins." Curious, in spite of himself, he glanced at her. "Do you have children?"

To his surprise, a pink blush appeared on her cheeks. "No. Trevor wasn't the type for fatherhood. But I'm hoping I'll be a mother someday. What about you— do you have children?"

He chuckled. "Not any that I know of."

She didn't reply, but the scornful expression on her face spoke volumes.

"I'm teasing," he felt inclined to say. "I don't have any children. And I don't plan on having any. I have plenty of four-legged babies to keep me happy."

She cut him another dry glance. "At least you know to stick to your calling."

If any other woman had said such a thing to him, he would've laughed. But hearing it from this blond beauty was altogether different. For some reason, it made him feel small and sleazy.

"At least I know my calling," he agreed. "Do you?"

"What is that supposed to mean?"

Suddenly Blake's voice was back in his head, reminding him to be nice to Isabelle. But damn it, Blake wasn't the one dealing with the woman. Holt was. And with each passing minute, she was getting deeper and deeper under his skin.

"I'm wondering if you've really thought about what you're taking on. Raising horses isn't an easy job."

"If it was easy, it wouldn't be rewarding, now would it?" she asked. "And I know all about hard work."

The sweetness in her voice was overlaid with conviction and Holt decided she was one of those stubborn females who'd rather die trying to prove a point than admit she might be wrong.

They reached the paddock and he opened a wide gate so the two of them could walk out to where the mares were munching hay from rows of mangers.

As they neared the horses, Holt pointed to one in particular. "I have one mare in this bunch that I'd be willing to part with and that's Blossom, the little chestnut over there with the star on her forehead and snip on her nose. She's made perfectly, I'd just prefer her to be a tad bigger. She was bred late—in May to be exact, so she should have a late April or early May baby."

"I'll go take a look."

They walked over to the mare and as she approached the horse for a closer look, Holt opened his mouth to remind her to be cautious, but instantly decided to keep the warning to himself. If Isabelle knew so much about horses, he shouldn't have to tell her a thing. This might be a good way to find out if she was the real deal or a woman with money and her head in the clouds.

Five minutes later, Holt had his answer. Blossom had not only forgotten the hay in front of her, she was nosing up to Isabelle as if they'd been friends forever. On top of that, the young mare had always been skittish about her feet, but Blossom had allowed Isabelle to pick up all four like she was a diva waiting for a manicure. It was amazing.

"She has a really nice eye and her teeth look good," she said as she dropped the mare's lip back in place.

"Chandler floats their teeth on a regular basis," he said, his green eyes dropping away from her hands and down to her rounded bottom encased in faded denim. Yesterday he'd been too tired and annoyed to notice Isabelle's perfect figure. This morning he was having trouble keeping his attention away from it.

She turned to face him and Holt jerked up his gaze before she caught him staring at her cute little butt.

"What sort of sire is this mare bred to?"

"The ranch's foundation stud. He's black and big boned. I'll show him to you after we look at the other mares."

She smiled and Holt's attention was drawn to the alluring sight of soft pink lips against white teeth. And suddenly he was wondering how she would look naked and lying next to him with her hair spilled over his shoulder.

"I look forward to seeing him," she said.

"So what do you think of Blossom?"

"She's nice. But I need to see the others before I make any kind of decision. Okay?"

Another smile softened her words and Holt felt his resistance crumbling like a shortbread cookie. Any man with half a brain could see she was a heartbreaker. But why should he let that put him off? He never made the mistake of letting a woman get near his heart. He enjoyed them for a while and then moved on. Isabelle was no different than the last beauty to warm his bed.

"Certainly," he answered. "Let's go find a truck and we'll drive out to the horse pasture."

Throughout the short trip to the pasture, Isabelle tried to ignore Holt's presence in the cab of the truck, but the more she tried to dismiss him, the more suffocated she felt. Back at the ranch yard, he'd wrapped a hand around her arm to assist her climb into the tall work truck, and even through the quilted thickness of her coat, the touch of his fingers had left a burning imprint.

But that was hardly a surprise. Everything about the man, from his sauntering walk to the growl in his voice, shouted sex. Or was he really no different than any other man she'd ever met? Could the long months of a cold, empty bed be causing her to see him in a different light?

Whatever the reason for her ridiculous reaction to the man, she needed to get over it and quick. There was no way she could make a smart business transaction when her mind was preoccupied with how he'd look with his shirt off, or wonder how it would feel to have those strong arms wrapped around her.

Damn it! She didn't need a man. Not

now. And definitely not a Romeo in cowboy boots.

"I've not been here long enough to learn about your weather," she said, hoping to push her thoughts to a safer place. "Is it usually this cool in January? I was hoping that this part of the state was southern enough to miss the cold and snow."

"Other than a few rare flurries blowing in the wind, you won't see snow around here," he answered. "But it can get fairly cold. Especially at night. What little rain we do get comes in the winter months. I hope you have plenty of water sources on your ranch. Otherwise, when the dry months come, you're going to be in trouble."

Did the man think she'd gotten to Arizona on the back of a turnip truck? Or was he doubting her common sense because she was a woman? Either way, he seemed intent on insulting her intelligence.

But she was trying her best to ignore his

remarks, the same way she was trying to dismiss the way his chin jutted slightly forward and the rusty stubble on his face had grown even longer since she'd seen him yesterday morning. Normally she had an aversion to men who didn't keep their faces clean-shaven. But there was something very earthy and sexy about the way the whiskers outlined his square jaw and firm lips.

She cleared her throat and said, "I made sure about the water supply before I purchased the property. And I've had enough firewood hauled in for the fireplace to last through the winter. I have fifty tons of Tifton/alfalfa in the hay barn and enough grain to last a month. In spite of what you might think of me, I do know how to make preparations."

He glanced at her and grinned. "I'm glad to hear you're prepared. And, by the way, how do you know what I'm thinking of you?"

She bit back a groan and decided the

best way to deal with this man was to be forthright. Lifting her chin, she said, "It's fairly obvious you think I'm an idiot. I'm not sure why you've put me in that category, but you have. And I'm trying not to let it bother me. After all, I think you're a bit of an arrogant brute. So there—we're even."

Expecting him to be peeved with her, she was totally surprised when he let out a hearty laugh. "An arrogant brute, eh? I've been called plenty of things before, but never that one." He directed another lopsided grin in her direction. "And you have me all wrong, Isabelle. I hardly think you're an idiot. I merely think you might be biting off more than you can chew."

"Because I'm a woman?"

He shook his head. "No. Because you're clearly chasing a dream. Instead of facing the hard work in front of you."

She wanted to be angry with him. She wanted to tell him that a person without dreams wasn't really living. But she stifled both urges. There had already been too many personal exchanges between the two of them and it was beginning to make her feel uncomfortable. It was making her think of him as a man rather than a neighbor or horse trainer. And that was something that could only lead to trouble.

"I know all about hard work, Mr. Hollister," she said stiffly.

"Please call me Holt."

She rolled her eyes in his direction to see the grin on his face was still there. Five minutes with Holt Hollister was really too much for any woman to endure and hold on to her sanity, she decided.

He steered the truck off the beaten dirt track and braked it to a stop near a wide galvanized gate. Beyond the fence, Isabelle could see thirty or more head of horses milling around a cluster of long wooden feed troughs.

"Here we are," he announced. "And fortunately, the horses are still at their feed.

I think there are thirty-five head in this herd."

Purposely keeping her gaze on the horses, she asked, "How many of these are for sale?"

"Four. I'll take a halter with me so you can take your time with each one."

"Thanks. I'd appreciate that."

They left the truck and after he collected a halter from the back, they walked over to the fence. While he slipped the latch on the gate, she said, "I thought you were in the business of selling horses. Why the limit of four or five?"

"This past year, we had to take several horses out of the working remuda for different reasons, such as lameness and age and so forth. And then Blake decided to add more cattle to our ranch down at Dragoon, so I've had to send more horses for the hands to use down there. Replacing them takes time and lots of training. So I'm actually running a bit short on older horses and somewhat short on the year-lings."

He followed her into the pasture and as Isabelle watched him carefully fasten the gate behind them, she realized that for once in her life, she was just as interested in looking at a man as she was a herd of horses.

"I see. I was thinking you might just limit the buyers who have their heads in the clouds."

He chuckled and Isabelle decided an arrogant brute who could laugh at himself couldn't be all bad.

"Not at all," he assured her. "I have special deals for those buyers."

Her laugh was shrewd. "I'll just bet you do."

Chapter Three

Over an hour later, Holt and Isabelle were back in the horse barn, where Holt had just finished showing her Hez A Rocket, the ranch's foundation stallion. She'd seemed very impressed with the animal, but Holt got the feeling she wasn't that enthralled with him.

And why would you want her to be, Holt? Right off the top of your head, you can probably think of four or five blond beauties who'd be happy to get a call from you. The last thing you need is a divorcée with a head full of dreams.

Holt purposely blocked out the voice of warning in his head as the two of them strolled in the general direction of his office. "Now that you've seen what I have to offer, are you ready to make a deal on one, or all?"

"Yes, I would. I—" She broke off as an ear-splitting whinny reverberated through the barn. "Wow! Someone wants attention. That sounds like another stallion."

Holt silently groaned. She'd told him her dream was to find a blue roan stallion and build her herd around him. Blue Midnight definitely fit her wishes, but Holt was grooming the young stud to replace Hez A Rocket in a few years. He'd never put the young stallion up for sale.

"That's Blue Midnight, one of my other stallions," he reluctantly admitted. "He can be quite a talker at times."

Her brows piqued with interest. "Blue? Is he a roan?"

With a resigned nod of his head, he said, "That's right. I was hoping to spare you from seeing him."

Confused by that, she asked, "Really? Why?"

"Because you're going to want him. And I'm going to have to say no and then you're going to be peeved at me—again."

"I really doubt that would ruin your day." She smiled and shrugged. "I've been told no plenty of times. I won't burst into tears—unless you refuse to let me see this super stud."

He shook his head. "You get a kick out of looking at a piece of pie even though you can't eat it?"

"I can always dream."

He should've seen that coming, Holt thought. "Ah, that's right," he said wryly. "You are fond of dreaming."

Taking her by the arm, he led her across the wide alleyway and past three empty stalls until they were standing in front of Blue Midnight's roomy compartment. Always eager for company, the horse hung his head over the top of the mesh iron gate and nickered softly at the two of them.

"Oh! Oh, Holt, he's gorgeous! Absolutely gorgeous! His hair is so slick and shiny! You must be keeping him blanketed."

Holt glanced over to see an incredible glow had come over Isabelle's face. As though storm clouds had parted above her head and golden sunshine was pouring over her. He'd put some happy faces on a few women before, but none of those blissful looks compared to what he was seeing on Isabelle's lovely features.

"No blankets. Blue Midnight is naturally tight haired. He just turned four and I have to admit, he's my pride and joy."

"Most stallions bite. Does he?"

"Not this one. He's very sweet natured."

She stepped up to the gate and quickly made friends with the horse. As she gently stroked his nose, she glanced over her shoulder and gave Holt a beseeching smile.

"Are you sure you don't want to sell him?" she asked. "I'd give you top dollar. Just name your price. If I don't have enough money, I'll get the money."

From her rich ex-husband? The notion left a bitter taste in Holt's mouth and for one split second he wanted to tell her that if she'd keep smiling at him the way she was smiling right now, he'd give her the world and Blue Midnight with it. But thankfully, the urge only lasted a second before sanity stepped in and reminded him that pleasing a woman didn't require losing his mind and his best stallion with it.

"Sorry," he told her. "I have big plans for this guy and they're all right here on Three Rivers."

"Oh, I'm sorry, too." Disappointment chased all the lovely glow from her face and she turned back to Blue Midnight and rubbed her cheek against his. "You're such a pretty boy," she said to the horse.

"I wish you could be mine. We'd be great buddies."

The interchange between her and the horse was something so palpable and real that Holt felt like an outsider listening in on a very private conversation.

Clearing his throat, he stepped forward until he was standing at her side. Immediately, the sweet scent of her drifted to his nostrils and pushed away the smells of alfalfa, dust, and manure.

"Blue Midnight has a few babies coming later this spring. If one of them turns out to be a colt, I'll sell him to you."

She looked over at him and Holt was stunned to see a sheen of tears in her blue eyes. He realized he was denying this woman her most fervent wish, but mixing sentimentality with business never worked. Neither did getting dopey over a woman he'd just met.

"Is that a promise?" she asked, her gaze searching his.

Aside from his mother or sisters, Holt

didn't make promises to women. But something about Isabelle's blue eyes was dissolving that rule.

"I wouldn't have said it if I hadn't meant it," he answered.

Her gaze turned back to Blue Midnight, who was gently nudging her shoulder for more attention.

"Thank you, Holt. I'll hold on to that promise."

After a couple more minutes with Blue Midnight, they returned to his office. A half hour later, she was using her phone to transfer money from her bank to a Three Rivers' account.

"You didn't have to take all five of them, Isabelle. Unless you really wanted to."

"I wanted to." She slipped the phone back into her handbag. "When will be a convenient time for me to come back with my trailer and pick them up?"

Holt wrote out a paper receipt, then went over to one of the many file cabinets lined against the wall. "No need for that," he told her. "Myself or some of the hands will deliver them. After what you paid for the five mares, it's the least I can do."

He flipped through several folders before he finally found what he was looking for. Back at his desk, he signed the transfers and placed them, the receipt, and the registration papers in a long envelope and handed it to Isabelle.

"Here's all the paperwork. If you have any problems changing the ownership into your name, just let me know. I hope you'll be happy with the mares, Isabelle."

She stood and reached across the desktop to shake his hand. "Thank you, Holt. It's been a pleasure."

Holt rose and clasped his hand around hers. "A pleasure?" he asked wryly. "Dealing with an arrogant brute?"

A pretty pink color touched her cheeks and Holt was charmed even more by her modesty. He couldn't remember making any of his old girlfriends blush, but then none of them could be labeled modest.

"You made up for it. Especially with letting me meet Blue Midnight."

"Good. Because I'd like for us to be friends."

She pulled her hand from his and reached for her handbag on the floor. "I thought we'd already become friends."

He moved around the desk and stood in front of her. "We have. I only meant, uh, that I want us to be closer friends. The kind that have dinner together. What do you say?"

Her eyes wide with disbelief, she looked up at him. "Are you inviting me on a date?"

She made it sound like he was suggesting the two of them make a lunar landing. "That's right. Nothing dangerous. Just a nice meal and some conversation."

Who are you trying to fool, Holt? For you, conversation with a woman is merely a means to an end. Just a step in the game of seduction. And once you do seduce Isabelle, then what? Is she the type you can brush aside like a pesky fly? You'd better think twice about this one, cowboy.

While he tried to ignore the taunting voice in his head, she said, "To be honest, I've not done any dating since my divorce. I'm not sure I'm ready to get back into that sort of thing."

That hardly sounded encouraging, Holt thought. But perhaps she meant dating in a serious way. If so, then the two of them would make a perfect couple. If there was one word in the dictionary that Holt tried his best to avoid in the presence of a woman, it was *serious.*

"Why?" he asked. "Is your heart too broken to enjoy an evening out with a man?"

She looked away from him and cleared her throat. "Do you think that's any of your business?"

She was his business. When and why he'd decided that, he didn't know. He only knew that at some point between eating pastries with her earlier this morning and making the final deal for the mares a few minutes ago, he'd become slightly infatuated with her.

"Probably not. But I'm a curious kind of guy. And I figured if I asked, you'd tell me."

She rolled her eyes and then her lips began to twitch as she fought off a smile. "Okay, since you asked, I'll tell you. I'm not carrying a torch for Trevor. My choice to stay away from dating is more about keeping myself on course with more important things."

"And having a man in your life isn't important?"

"No. And I'm not sure it will ever be important again. Not unless some incredible superman comes along. And I can't see that happening."

No. Holt couldn't see that happening either. The only superman he'd ever known was his father and he'd died several years ago.

"Sorry. Most of us guys do have faults," he said. "But I'll do my best to keep them to a minimum for one night. That is, if you're willing to spend an evening with me."

She laughed and Holt was surprised at how relieved he was to hear the sound. Normally, he didn't give a whit whether a woman turned him down. There was always another one waiting. But Isabelle was different.

"All right. I'll have dinner with you—sometime," she told him.

"Sometime? No. I'm talking about tomorrow night. I'll pick you up at six."

She placed the envelope filled with the horse papers into her handbag and pulled the strap onto her shoulder. "I might have something else to do tomorrow night."

He gave her a pointed grin. "Like feed the horses? You can let the hands do that."

She held up her hands. "These are the only hands I have."

"Oh. Then I'll come early and help you."

"Persistent, aren't you?"

"When something is important to me."

She looked at him for a long moment, then turned and started out of the office. Holt followed after her.

"Okay, I'll be ready. At six." At the door, she paused and looked back at him. "Goodbye, Holt. And thank you."

He clasped a hand around her elbow. "I'll walk you to your truck."

"That isn't necessary."

"I wasn't thinking it was a necessity. More like a pleasure."

Shaking her head, she said, "I have to say, when your older brother promised me you'd be in a better humor today, he wasn't kidding. What did he do? Give you some sort of nice pill this morning?"

Holt laughed as he ushered her through the doorway. "Isabelle, I have a feeling we're going to be more than just friends. We're going to be great friends."

The next morning Isabelle was out stretching barbed wire on a fence close to the barn when she heard the rattle of a livestock trailer.

Unfastening the stretcher from the wire, she allowed the heavy tool to fall to the ground, then turned and, shading her eyes, watched as a truck and trailer barreled up the dirt road that led to her ranch yard.

Was that Holt delivering her horses?

The mere thought that the driver of the big black ton truck might be the sexy horse trainer was enough to cause her pulse to quicken, but as she began walking in the direction of the barn, she determinedly kept her stride at a normal pace. If Holt was behind the wheel, she hardly wanted him to think she was eager to see him.

Still, she paused long enough to wipe

her palms down the front of her jeans and smooth back the loose tendrils of hair that had escaped her ponytail. As for the long streak of grease on the front of her flannel shirt, there was nothing she could do about that.

However, by the time Isabelle reached the barn area, she realized all her preening had been for nothing. Instead of Holt climbing out of the truck, she spotted a pair of Three River Ranch hands. One was burly with red hair while his tall, lanky partner appeared to be much younger.

The older one of the pair was the first to introduce himself. "Hello, Ms. Townsend. I'm Pat," he said, then jerked a thumb toward the man standing next to him. "And this is Cott. We do day work for Three Rivers Ranch. Holt sent us over with your mares."

Disappointment rippled through her. Which was a totally silly reaction, she thought. He'd only suggested he might deliver the horses himself, he hadn't made it a promise. Still, it would've been kinda nice if he'd taken the time out of his busy morning to deliver the mares personally.

"Nice to meet you, Pat and Cott. Thanks for bringing the mares. If you'll follow me in the truck, I'll open the gates for you."

A few minutes later, the horses were bucking and running around the wooden corral, sending a huge cloud of dust billowing into the air. The sight of their excited antics caused Isabelle to laugh out loud.

"They're feeling good, Ms. Townsend," Pat said as he and Cott joined her outside the corral gate.

"I'm very happy to get them," she said, then politely offered, "Would you guys like something to drink? A cold bottle of water or lemonade? Sorry, but I don't have any beer."

"Thanks, but we're fine. We have water in the truck," Pat told her. "If you'll just show us where you want the feed unloaded, we'll be on our way."

Isabelle stared at him. "Excuse me? Did you say feed?"

Cott answered, "That's right. Two tons of horse feed. It's Three Rivers' special mix. Or I guess I should say Holt's special mix. He's the one who originally concocted it."

She shook her head. "But I didn't purchase any feed from the ranch. Only the mares."

"No matter, Ms. Townsend," Cott replied. "Holt said to bring it to you and what he says goes."

Holt said. Holt said.

Just what was he trying to say to Isabelle? That much high-quality feed would be worth hundreds of dollars. Was he trying to butter her up?

She was being stupid. A man like him didn't need to score points with her, or any woman. She figured this was more about being concerned for the mares. Abruptly changing a horse's feed often caused serious health issues with their digestive track. Mixing the Three Rivers feed with hers would allow her to easily make the gradual change.

Realizing the men were waiting on her response, she gestured toward the far end of the big barn. "Okay. My feed room is around at the back of the barn. Follow me and I'll show you the way."

With the two men working in tandem, they had the stacks of fifty-pound sacks unloaded in no time. After Isabelle had thanked them and they'd driven away, she went straight to the house, where she'd left her cell phone on the kitchen counter.

A quick glance at the face told her she had two new text messages. One from her mother, who lived in San Diego, the other from Holt.

She punched Holt's open first and read: Sorry I couldn't make it with the mares. I'll see you tonight at six.

Tonight at six. The reminder caused her heart to thump hard in her chest.

What was the matter with her? Only

two days before, she'd wanted Holt Hollister to jump off the rim of the Grand Canyon. How had she gone from that to agreeing to go on a date with the man? Sure, he'd been charming yesterday. But her failed marriage had left her emotionally drained. She had nothing to offer any man.

Deciding Holt's message didn't require a response, she opened the one from her mother.

I've managed to snag a showing at the Westside Gallery! Call me when you have a minute.

As far as Isabelle knew, Gabby Townsend had never had a one-minute conversation in her entire life. Especially when she got on the phone with her one and only child. But Isabelle hadn't talked with her mother in the past few days and now was just as good a time as later to call her.

Grabbing a bottle of water from the

fridge, Isabelle downed a hefty drink, then sat down at the kitchen table with her phone.

"Issy, honey," her mother answered. "Can you believe my work is going to be shown at the Westside Gallery?"

The excitement in her mother's voice caused Isabelle to smile. "I absolutely can believe it. Your artwork is fabulous, Mom. It deserves to be shown to the public."

"That's what Carl said. Actually he was just as impressed with my charcoals as he was my oils, so both are going to be displayed. It's incredible!" Pausing, she let out a breathless little laugh. "I guess you can tell I'm walking on air."

"Just a bit," Isabelle said. "But you deserve to feel that way, Mom. Uh, who is this Carl? Do I know him?"

"I don't think so, dear. Carl Whitaker is the owner of the gallery. I met him a couple of weeks ago at the Green Garden Winery. Caprice has a few of my paintings on her walls there and Carl spotted them. You remember the Green Garden, don't you? That's where that suave Italian businessman tried to pick you up."

Isabelle remembered, all right. He'd been good-looking and wealthy to boot. But she'd been turned off by his constant boasting and sleazy looks.

"You mean that snake wearing alligator shoes? I try to forget those kinds of encounters."

"If you'd cozied up to him, you might be relaxing in a Mediterranean villa about now," Gabby suggested slyly.

"I'd rather jump into quicksand with concrete blocks tied to my feet."

Gabby groaned, then said, "I don't want you to get involved with a creep, but I do wish you'd take an interest in men again. It just isn't right for you to be alone."

For some odd reason, her mother's remark caused Holt's rugged face to appear in front of her vision and she promptly tried to blink it away.

"You're alone, Mom."

"That's different," Gabby said. "I'm sixty-three. I've already done the marriage-baby thing. You have your whole life ahead of you."

Isabelle grimaced. "You're not exactly over the hill, Mom. And I've already gone through the marriage thing, too. Remember?"

Her mother's short sigh was full of frustration. "Issy, your marriage—"

After a long pause, Isabelle wanted to butt in and change the subject, but she'd learned long ago that trying to steer her mother was like trying to make a cat obey commands. The task was pretty much impossible.

Finally, Gabby said, "Yours wasn't a real marriage."

Bemused by that remark, Isabelle pulled the phone away from her ear and stared at it for a brief second before she slapped it back to the side of her head. "Excuse me, Mom, but it was real to me."

"If it was so real, then why did you divorce?"

Isabelle let out a long, weary breath. She'd not planned to get into this sort of conversation with her mother today. In fact, it had been ages since Gabby had brought up anything about Isabelle's divorce.

"Okay, Mom, let me rephrase that. It was real on my part. For Trevor, I was just an enjoyable companion."

"Oh, honey—well, at least you didn't have a baby."

Isabelle pressed a hand to her forehead and closed her eyes. "Thanks, Mom. That reminder makes me feel great."

"Isabelle, you know what I mean. It's terrible when a child is passed back and forth between parents—just because the parents can't cohabitate. Just look at your own parents. Look what it did to you."

Isabelle's parents had divorced while she'd been in middle school. And back then, she would've been lying if she said it hadn't upended her life. She'd loved her father dearly and when he'd moved out of the house, she'd felt like he'd deserted her and her mother. She'd been too young to fully understand that her parents had divorced because they'd been two different souls, both wanting and needing different things in life.

"It hurt for a while. But I think I turned out fairly normal."

Gabby said gently, "You're better than normal. Especially with having a pair of hippies for parents."

Isabelle chuckled. "You and Dad aren't hippies. You're free spirits."

"Aww, that's a sweet way of putting it, honey. Most of our friends would describe us as harebrained or worse."

"Who cares? As long as you're both happy."

"I'm certainly happy. And I think your father is, too. The last I talked with him, he was in New Orleans playing nightly on Bourbon Street."

Her father, Nolan, was an accomplished pianist. Twenty years ago, he'd helped to form a small jazz band. Since then, the group had traveled all over the country playing small venues. He'd made a decent living at his profession, but like Gabby, his craft was really all he cared about. As long as he was making music, he was happy.

"Hmm. A dream gig for him," Isabelle replied. "I haven't talked with him in a while. I'll give him a call soon."

"He'd like that."

Once again, Holt's image swaggered across her mind's eye and the unexpected distraction caused her to pause long enough to cause her mother concern.

"Issy, is something wrong? Have you quarreled with your father?"

"No. Nothing is wrong. Actually, I was thinking about someone," she admitted. "Believe it or not, I'm going on a date tonight."

Gabby reacted with a long stretch of silence.

"Mom, are you still there? Or have you fallen over in a dead faint?"

Gabby laughed softly. "I'm still conscious. Just a bit surprised."

Isabelle said, "I'm surprised at myself. I'm having dinner with the rancher that sold horses to me. It's just sort of a thank-you date on both sides. Him for selling and me for buying."

"Oh. Sure, I see. It's really a business dinner or…something like that."

Business? Isabelle could hardly look across the table at Holt and think business. In fact, she doubted she'd be able to think about much at all. But her mother didn't need to know her daughter was looking at any man in such an intimate way.

"I'm very happy for you, Mom. Maybe you'll sell a few things and you can book that trip to Hawaii you've been wanting to take."

"I'm not really worried so much about selling right now. I'm just happy to have my work exhibited in such a notable gallery. The rest will take care of itself," she said, then asked, "Will you be able to come down on the opening day? I'll be there to meet and greet and the gallery is supplying refreshments."

"When is this happening?"

"Two weeks from this coming Saturday. Don't worry. I'll remind you."

"I'll try. But I can't make any promises. It all depends if I can hire a couple of hands between now and then. Until someone is here to care for the horses, I can't leave the ranch for more than a few hours at a time."

"Have you advertised for help?"

"I don't want to go that route. I'm afraid I'd have all sorts of creeps coming out here to the ranch. Before I hire anyone, I'm going to ask around and get some recommendations."

"I understand. Don't worry about the

showing. You have your hands full right now. We'll get together later on."

"I'd love that, Mom. Now, I've got to hang up and get back to my fence repairs."

Gabby let out a good-natured groan. "My beautiful little girl out building fence instead of making use of her college degree."

"I'm happier now than I've ever been."

"You're just as much of a free spirit as your parents," she said gently. "And that's okay, too. Perhaps you can talk the rancher into helping you with the fence."

Holt Hollister stretching barbed wire? He was ranching royalty, a boss on one of the largest ranches in the state of Arizona. Isabelle seriously doubted he'd ever touched a posthole digger or a roll of wire.

"I can't talk that fast, Mom," Isabelle said with a laugh.

"Then add a little wink or two between words," Gabby suggested.

"Uh, if you knew what this guy looked

like you wouldn't be giving me that kind of advice."

"Why? Ugly as sin?"

"No. Sinfully handsome."

"Oh," she drawled in a suggestive tone. "I need to hear more about this man."

Isabelle chuckled. "Bye, Mom. I'll call you soon."

"Isabelle—"

"Yes?"

"I'll keep my fingers crossed for you, honey."

Gabby ended the call and Isabelle put down the phone, but she didn't immediately leave the chair. Instead, she sat there thinking about Holt and their date tonight. She'd only agreed to go out with him so she could bend his ear about the horse breeding business, she told herself. And for no other reason.

Next time she talked to her mother, she'd explain the situation. For now it wouldn't hurt to let Gabby believe her daughter was interested in finding a man to love.

Chapter Four

Holt couldn't remember the last time he'd been anywhere near the old Landry Ranch. Not since the family had moved to Idaho several years ago and put the property on the market. Holt had practically forgotten all about the deserted ranch. Until Isabelle had shown up on Three Rivers and Blake had informed him that she'd purchased the place.

Located about eighteen miles north of Three Rivers by way of a ten-mile stretch of narrow asphalt, plus eight more miles of rough, graveled road, the land butted up to only a half-mile section of Three Rivers' land. But that was enough for the Hollisters to consider the owner a neighbor.

Before he'd left home this evening, Holt had been about to step out the door when Blake had caught up to him. Seeing his brother had been curious as to where he was going on a weeknight, Holt had explained he was having dinner with Isabelle. In response, Blake had barely lifted an eyebrow.

I didn't figure you'd waste any time trying to get her into your bed, he'd said.

Ordinarily, Blake's coarse comment would've elicited a laugh from Holt. But Holt hadn't laughed. In fact, he'd felt strangely annoyed at his brother. Blake didn't really know Isabelle and to imply she was an easy girl had hardly been fair. But Holt figured his brother's remark had been more directed at him than at Isabelle.

The road he was traveling climbed a hill covered with agave and century plants, then curved abruptly to the right through spires of rock formation. After another curve in the opposite direction, the landscape opened up and far to his left he could see the house and the nearby cluster of barns and work sheds.

Holt remembered the ranch being in a beautiful area of Yavapai County, but until this moment he'd never really thought about how isolated the property was from neighbors or town. The idea of a tiny thing like Isabelle living out here alone left him uneasy. But then, she wasn't his responsibility. And how she chose to live was nobody's business but her own.

He'd barely had time to stop the truck in front of the hacienda-style house when he spotted Isabelle emerging from the front door. The sight of her jolted him and for a moment after he'd killed the motor, he sat there watching her walk to the edge of the porch.

She was wearing a black sweater dress that stopped just above her knees. The fabric clung to the curves of her body, while black dress boots outlined her shapely calves. Her blond hair was brushed to one side and waved against the side of her face. She looked sexy as hell and he wondered how he was supposed to eat a bite of food with that sort of temptation sitting across from him.

Collecting the flat box from the passenger seat, he left the truck and walked to the porch where she waited for him.

"Hello, Holt," she greeted. "I see you found the place."

The smile on her face was like sunshine on a spring day and it sent his spirit soaring.

"It wasn't hard. I've been here a few times. Back when the Landrys still lived here." He offered the box to her. "Here's a little something for you."

She took the fancy chocolates. "Thank

you, Holt. This should keep up my energy."

He grinned. "I figured with all those extra horses you bought from me, you'd need it."

She gestured to the door behind her. "Would you like to come in and have a drink before we go?"

"That would be nice. We have plenty of time to make our dinner reservations."

She tossed him a wary glance before moving toward the front door. "You made reservations?"

"That's what I normally do when I go out to eat. Don't you?" he asked, as he followed her over the threshold and down a short, wide foyer decorated with potted succulents and a wooden parson's bench.

"No. I normally go to a fast-food joint. Or a café where you simply walk in and sit wherever you'd like."

They entered a long living area and Isabelle walked over and placed the box of chocolates on a dark oak coffee table.

"Well, I do that sort of thing with my buddies or my brothers," he admitted, then grinned at her. "If I took you out for a hot dog, you might think I was cheap."

She walked back over to where he stood and Holt was once again staggered by the incredible smoothness of her skin, the vivid blue of her eyes. He'd heard the term *breathtaking* used many a time, but he'd never experienced it until he laid his eyes on Isabelle.

"As long as there's good conversation to go with the hot dog, I'd be happy."

Was she really that easy to please? She didn't look like a simple woman, he thought. But then, she didn't look like a hardworking horsewoman either. "I'll try to remember that."

An impish little smile played around her lips as she gestured to a long, moss green couch.

"Have a seat," she invited, "and I'll get the drinks. What would you like? Something alcoholic or a soft drink?"

Deciding he'd be able to breathe a bit better if he put some distance between them, he walked over and took a seat on the end of the couch, then crossed his boots out in front of him. "I'd really like a bourbon and Coke, but since I'm driving, a soft drink will do."

"I'll be right back," she told him.

She disappeared through an arched doorway and Holt glanced curiously around the long living room. He decided there was nothing frilly or overly feminine in Isabelle's taste. The furniture was solid and comfortable and all done in rich earth tones of greens and browns and yellows. Braided rugs added a splash of color to the dark hardwood floors. A TV filled one corner, while a tall bookshelf filled another, and though he was only guessing, Holt figured Isabelle reached for a book far more than she reached for the TV remote.

At the front of the room, a large picture window looked out at a distant cluster of hills dotted with cacti and rock formations. Since there were no curtains or blinds, Holt figured she either appreciated the view or enjoyed the sunshine streaming into the room or both.

The click of her high-heeled boots announced her return and he looked around to see her approaching with a glass of iced cola in each hand.

"Thank you," he said, taking the glass she offered.

"Would you like a chocolate to go with your soda?"

"No, thanks. I don't want to ruin my appetite."

She took a seat on the opposite end of the couch and carefully adjusted the hem of her dress toward her knees. The action drew Holt's attention to the shape of her legs and he found himself imagining what her thighs would feel like wrapped around his hips. Even though she was small, he had the feeling she'd be a strong lover.

One that would look him boldly in the eye and dare him to thrill her.

"I'm glad I got this chance to talk with you before we left for dinner," she said.

Her voice jerked him out of the erotic daydreams and as he looked at her, he hoped to heck she couldn't read his mind.

"Pardon me, but what can we talk about here that we can't talk about later?"

"The feed you sent over with the mares. I need to pay you for it."

"The grain was a bonus that went with the mares. I won't accept pay for the feed."

She grimaced and looked away from him. "That makes me feel…very uncomfortable."

"Why? I've thrown in extras on other horse deals." Which was true, he thought. But he'd never given anyone else as much as he'd given her. The feed was something they mixed for their own use on Three Rivers. It wasn't sold or given to anyone. Until Holt had broken the rules this morning and sent her two tons of it.

But she didn't need to know any of that. Nor did she need to know Blake had been a bit peeved at Holt's unusual generosity.

"I'm sorry you feel that way," he said. "It was meant to help you and the mares."

She leveled him with a pointed look. "And that's all?"

"What else?" he asked.

Through narrowed eyes, he watched her nervously lick her lips.

"Nothing, I suppose." She shrugged and glanced down at her drink. "I just don't like feeling beholden to anyone."

So she didn't want to owe him anything. Holt could understand her feelings. What he couldn't understand was how this woman affected him, how much he'd like for her to depend on him for advice and help and whatever else she needed. Which made no sense at all.

"That wasn't my intention," he said. "In case you hadn't noticed, I care deeply about my horses and even after they no longer belong to me, I want to know they're well taken care of. The feed was to help them make the transition from Three Rivers to here. It wasn't some sort of bribe for romantic favors. If that's what you were thinking."

The compression of her lips coupled with the bright pink color on her cheeks told Holt she was more than embarrassed; she was also annoyed.

"That wasn't what I was implying— well, not exactly," she said stiffly. "Anyway, I honestly doubt you need to play such silly games with the women you date."

Silly games? His sister Vivian had often accused him of playing women for fools. But that wasn't true. He never tried to manipulate a woman's feelings. That would be like trying to ride a horse without a bridle. It wasn't an impossible task, but it would take way more patience and time than he had.

He shook his head. "It's obvious you've

already heard gossip about me. That I'm a playboy or worse."

The color on her face turned a deeper shade. "Believe me, Holt, whether you're a playboy or not means little to me. What you do with your private life is your business. You and I are just having dinner. That's all."

Just dinner. That's all he wanted, too, Holt thought. Having anything more to do with this woman would be inviting trouble. The kind he didn't need.

In spite of feeling oddly deflated, he smiled at her. "I'm glad we got all of that behind us. So if you're ready, I think we should be leaving. The drive to the restaurant takes a while."

Appearing relieved by his suggestion, she rose to her feet. "Certainly. Just let me get my bag and coat."

While she gathered her things from a nearby chair, Holt placed his empty glass on the coffee table and left the couch to join her. As he helped her slip into the coat, he was stuck by her flowery scent and small, vulnerable size. He could swing her into his arms without any effort at all. And with the silence of the house surrounding them, he could easily imagine himself carrying her to bed.

Dinner is what this evening is about, Holt. Remember? Not sex or drama or stifling strings or a broken heart.

And why the heck should his heart get involved if he took this woman to bed? He practically yelled the retort back at the negative voice going off in his head. He was thirty-three years old and he'd never made the mistake of falling in love. It wasn't going to happen to him. Not now. Not ever. He had nothing to worry about.

As Holt drove the two of them away from the ranch, Isabelle studied him from the corner of her eye. She couldn't deny he looked incredibly handsome tonight in a white shirt and dark Western-cut slacks. A bolo tie with a slide fashioned of onyx and silver was pushed almost to the top button, which had been left open. The black cowboy hat settled low on his forehead was made of incredibly smooth felt, the sort that cost a fortune. But the price of the hat was probably only a fraction of what he'd paid for the fish-skin boots.

The fact that Holt Hollister was rich should have been a total turnoff. Once her divorce to Trevor had become final, she'd made a silent vow to never waste her time or emotions on a rich man. From her experience, a man with stacks of money was rarely the homey sort.

He glanced in her direction. "Pat and Cott tell me you're looking to hire some day workers."

While the two men had been unloading the feed, she'd mentioned she needed to find a couple of dependable ranch hands. Apparently they'd relayed the information to Holt.

"That's right. I need help with the heavier chores. Right now I'm repairing fence and it's a rather hard job to do with only one pair of hands."

He shook his head. "Building fence without help is asking for trouble."

"The way I see it, working with a pair of creeps trying to take advantage of me is more dangerous than building fence alone."

"Hmm. You do have a point there."

She looked out at the passing landscape. "Trevor left me pretty well set financially. But not well enough for me to pay two hefty salaries every month. I can't manage that until the ranch starts making a profit. Which won't be for a long time yet. Right now I'd be happy to find a pair of trustworthy wranglers willing to work a few hours a day."

"My family and I have plenty of connections. Maybe we can help you with that."

"I'd appreciate your help, Holt."

He glanced at her and grinned, and Isabelle thought how different he seemed

now from that first day she'd walked up
to him in the horse barn. He'd been cold
and abrupt and anything but charming.
The guy sitting next to her tonight had
to be the one that Emily-Ann had called
dreamy.

He asked, "Have you always been so
adventurous?"

"What do you mean?"

"Other than my mother, I can't think of
one woman who'd be brave enough or ambitious enough to take on the huge task of
starting a horse ranch. The idea of living
alone in an isolated area would be enough
to put most women off."

She didn't know whether he was giving
her a compliment or questioning her wis-
dom. But then, it didn't really matter what
this man thought of her. Did it?

"I've never been the timid sort. My
parents always taught me to follow my
dreams, no matter how big or daunting."

"What do your parents think about this
new endeavor of yours?"

"They're very supportive. Honestly, the idea of me failing at anything never crosses my father's mind. He, uh, sort of lives in his own little world. He's a musician, you see, and has played piano in a jazz band for more than twenty years. My mother believes in me, too. Except that sometimes she worries about me. She's a very open-minded person, but she has this old-fashioned notion that I'd be happier with a man in my life. Thankfully she'd doesn't pester me too much about it, though. With her being single herself, there's not much she can say."

He glanced curiously at her. "Your parents aren't together?"

"No. Not since I was a small girl. But they're still good friends."

"Hmm. Must be something that runs in your family."

"Divorce, you mean?"

"No. Being divorced friends. Like you and—what's his name?"

"Oh, like me and Trevor." She shrugged.

"I guess in that way I'm like my parents. Except that they had a child together. Trevor and I didn't. Which is a blessing— that's what Gabby thinks."

"Gabby?"

"That's my mother's name. Her real name is Gabrielle, but no one ever calls her that."

His expression turned thoughtful. "So Gabby is relieved you didn't have a child with this Trevor guy. Are you?"

"Am I what?"

"Relieved that you don't share a child with your ex."

He was getting too personal, but then she'd practically asked for it with all this chattering she'd been doing. Darn it, she'd been talking way too much. Because she was nervous, she silently reasoned with herself. Not because she found this man easy to talk to.

Shifting around in the seat, she tugged the hem of her dress closer to her knees. "*Relieved* is the wrong word, Holt. *Sad* is closer to it. I promised myself that whenever I had a child it would be with a man who loved me. Trevor didn't fall into that category."

A frown puckered his forehead. "You can tell me to mind my own business, but why did you marry him if you believed he didn't love you?"

He couldn't begin to know how many times she'd called herself a fool, or how often she'd questioned her hasty decision to marry. "We had a whirlwind courtship and when Trevor whisked me off to a wedding chapel in Las Vegas, it was all so romantic. It felt like love. Later on I learned differently."

"I see."

How could he see? He'd never been married. And from the vibes she'd been getting from him, she seriously doubted he'd ever been in love.

"You do?" she asked quietly.

"Sure. Your ex mostly wanted a pretty woman on his arm and in his bed. Now you want a real husband and children. But you aren't interested in dating. How's that going to work out?"

Her short laugh was a cynical sound. "I'm only twenty-eight. I have a few years before my childbearing days are over."

His only reaction to her answer was the slight arch of one brow, and Isabelle figured he was probably thinking she was impulsive and silly and not the sort of woman he'd ever want to get involved with. Well, that was good, she told herself. Because he was the sort of man who would never fit into her future plans.

Twenty miles and just as many minutes later, darkness had settled across the desert landscape and Holt turned off the main highway and onto a narrow asphalt road. As the truck began to climb into a forested mountain, Isabelle grew increasingly curious.

"Excuse me, Holt, but are you sure we're going to dinner? This looks more like we're on the road to a hunting cabin. I'm getting the feeling that our food is hanging from a hook and you're going to cook it over an open fire."

He laughed. "What little I can cook, you wouldn't want to eat. Trust me. We're going to have a regular sit-down dinner with glass plates and silverware. No throwaway plastic."

"Do you always go this far out of town to eat? Or are you just driving this far to avoid being seen with me in Wickenburg?"

He laughed again and the sexy sound slid down her backbone like the warm tip of a finger.

"Now, why wouldn't I want to be seen with you?"

"You might have lady friends there who wouldn't appreciate seeing you with me," she said shrewdly.

"That would be their problem, not mine," he said, then added, "Actually, I'm driving this far because the place is unique and I thought you might enjoy it. Plus the food is delicious. Their specialty is Italian, but they have American dishes on the menu, too."

"I'm not hard to please," she told him. "I would probably even eat whatever you cooked over the fire."

He chuckled. "Maybe I'll practice up and put you to the test sometime."

Holt had been right when he'd said the restaurant was unique. The gray stone structure resembled an English manor and was perched high on the edge of a mountain. Footlights were strategically placed on the grounds to illuminate the planked board entrance and a beautiful lawn that was canopied with tall pines and spruce.

"This is like a forested fairyland, Holt. It's…completely enchanting!"

"I'm glad you approve."

He helped her out of the truck, then tossed the keys to a waiting valet. Then curving an arm against her back, he urged her toward the main entrance.

Once inside, they were greeted by a young hostess. She promptly ushered them to a small, square table near a wall of plate glass.

After they were seated and the hostess had disappeared, Isabelle looked around in fascination at the sea of linen-covered tables, tall beamed ceilings, and intricate tiled floor. As Holt had suggested, it was unique and very special.

"Beyond the glass wall, there's a balcony with tables. Usually in the winter, they keep a fire going in the firepit. It's a nice place to have after-dinner coffee—if you'd like," he suggested.

"Sounds wonderful," she agreed, then asked, "What do you usually eat when you come here?"

"Steak." Chuckling, he attempted to defend his mundane choice. "What can I say? I'm a rancher. But I do usually get ravioli or spaghetti with it. That gets me a bit out of the box, doesn't it?"

She laughed. "The spaghetti alone puts you way out of the box."

A young waiter arrived with menus and Holt ordered a bottle of sparkling red wine. While they sipped and waited for the first course of their meal to be served, Isabelle did her best to keep the conversation on the safest subject she could think of, which in their case was raising horses. But after a while, she found herself wanting to know more about Holt Hollister the man, rather than the successful horse breeder.

Throughout the delicious dinner, she managed to tamp down the personal questions, but after they moved to a table on the balcony, her guard began to relax and before she knew it, she was encouraging him to talk about himself and his family.

"So you got your love of horses from your father?" she asked, as they enjoyed cups of rich, dark coffee.

Behind her, the crackling heat from the firepit warmed her back and cast an orange gold glow over Holt's rugged features. Nearby, in a ballroom attached to the balcony, music had begun to play and the occasional sound of laughter drifted out to them. The atmosphere was decidedly romantic, Isabelle thought, but she was trying hard not to focus on that part of the evening.

He nodded. "The first time Dad put me on a horse I was too small to walk. Mom said I screamed to the top of my lungs when the ride ended. Dad was a great horseman and I always wanted to be just like him."

"You must have achieved your goal. From what people around Wickenburg have told me, you're a regular horse whisperer."

Smiling modestly, he shook his head. "I might be good with horses, but I'll never be the man that Dad was."

She frowned. "You keep saying was. Isn't your father still living?"

For the first time since she'd met Holt, she saw an unmistakable look of sadness on his face.

"Dad—his name was Joel—died over six years ago. An incident with a horse. He was found with his boot hung in the stirrup. He'd been dragged—for a long distance."

She gasped. "Oh, how tragic, Holt. To lose him that way—I mean, to have his death connected to a horse—something he dearly loved. Something you dearly love. It's horrible."

He cleared his throat, then took a sip of coffee before he finally replied, "A horse didn't kill Dad."

Totally confused by his remark, she stared at him. "What?"

His gaze left her face and settled on the shadows beyond the balcony. "I shouldn't have said that. We—don't really know what happened to Dad. But we're pretty damned sure the horse didn't have anything to do with his death."

The tightness of his features told her there was much more to this story, more than he wanted to talk about. And it suddenly dawned on her that Holt Hollister might've been born into wealth, but his life hadn't been without heartache.

"Oh," she said. "Then you're thinking he must have had a heart attack or stroke or some sudden medical problem while he was out riding."

"That would be the logical deduction, but you're wrong. The autopsy showed no sign of any medical issue. Dad was in great health." He looked at her, his expression both bleak and frustrated. "At that time, the Yavapai County sheriff was a close friend of ours. He ruled Dad's death as an accident. Only because he didn't have enough evidence to prove otherwise. He passed away a few years ago from lung disease, or he would still be working on the case."

In spite of the fire behind her, she felt chilled. "Evidence? You mean—that someone—purposely harmed your father?"

He nodded. "That's what I'm saying. My brothers and I have been searching for answers all these years. We think we're getting close to finding out what really happened, but we need a few more pieces to put the whole puzzle together."

"I'm so sorry, Holt. I didn't realize your father was gone, much less that anything so—horrible had occurred. I'm sure it's not something you want to talk about."

He shrugged. "Sometimes it helps to talk about things that hurt."

Yes, like having a husband who hadn't loved her. Like desperately wanting children and not having any. Yes, she'd experienced things that hurt.

"What happened with the horse your father was riding?"

"Major Bob is still on the ranch," he said fondly. "Still being used in the working remuda. That's the way Dad would've wanted it. And once Major Bob grows old and dies, he'll be buried on the ranch next to Dad. They were great buddies."

"Like me and Albert." Tears suddenly filled her eyes and she blinked rapidly and reached for her coffee in an effort to hide them. "I'd like to see Major Bob and the rest of the remuda sometime. If that's possible." She gave him a wry smile. "I'm sure you've already come to the conclusion that I'm horse crazy. Or maybe just crazy in general."

"Not yet." He grinned and gestured toward her cup. "If you've had enough of coffee, let's walk over to the ballroom. It has a really nice dance floor."

Isabelle loved to dance. But she wasn't at all sure about taking a spin around the dance floor in Holt's arms. No. That wouldn't be smart, at all.

"I, uh, think I'd better pass on the dancing."

His eyes narrowed with speculation.

"Why? Scared you might miss a step and crush my toes?"

She purposely straightened her shoulders. "No. I'm not scared of missing a step. Anyway, I'm not heavy enough to crush your toes."

Laughing, he rose to his feet and reached for her hand. "Then I don't have a thing to worry about. And neither do you."

Deciding it would look silly to protest too much, she allowed him to pull her to her feet and lead her across the balcony.

As they entered the ballroom, the band began playing a slow ballad and Isabelle didn't have time to ready herself. He quickly pulled her into his arms and guided her among the group of dancers circling the floor.

Even if she'd had hours to brace herself, she wouldn't have been prepared for the onslaught of sensations rushing through her. Having his strong arm against her back and her hand clasped tightly in his was enough to cause her breathing to go haywire. But to have the front of his rock-hard body pressed to hers was totally shattering her senses.

"This is nice," he said. "Very nice."

His voice wasn't far from her ear and she knew if she turned her head slightly to the right, she'd be looking him square in the face. The thought of what that would do to her put a freeze on her neck muscles and kept her gaze fixed on a point of his shoulder.

"I've not danced in a long time," she admitted, hoping the sound of the music hid the husky tone of her voice. "I'm a little rusty."

He moved his hand ever so slightly against her back and she momentarily closed her eyes against the heat that was slowly and surely beginning to spread through her body.

"It's just like riding a horse," he murmured. "You get in rhythm and the rest comes naturally."

The man was undoubtedly a master at

the art of seduction and if she didn't do something and fast, she was going to become his next victim.

"I'm beginning to think I should have worn my boots and spurs," she said.

His fingers tightened around hers and she wondered why the touch of his hand felt so good against hers.

"You know what I'm beginning to think?" he asked.

"I won't try to guess."

"You're scared of me."

That was all it took to repair the paralysis in her neck and she turned her head until her gaze was locked with his.

Lifting her chin to a challenging angle, she said, "I'm not scared of anyone."

The corners of his lips tilted ever so slightly. "You think that's wise?"

Nothing about being with this man was wise. But it was darned thrilling. And every woman needed to be thrilled once in a while, she decided.

She said, "I'd rather be brave than wise.

Besides, I'm beginning to think you might just be a little afraid of me."

Amused by her remark, he grinned and Isabelle forced her gaze to remain boldly locked onto his.

"And why would I be afraid of you?" he asked.

She could feel her heart beating way too fast and hard. But with Holt's arms fastened around her, there was no way she could make her pulse settle back to a normal rhythm.

"You might get to liking me so much you'll decide to sell Blue Midnight to me," she answered.

Laughing, he pulled her even tighter against him. "Oh, Isabelle, this evening is turning out to be better than I could've ever imagined."

Her resistance a crumbling mess, Isabelle rested her cheek against his shoulder and promised herself that she had nothing to worry about. This was just one dance, Holt was just like any other man, and tomorrow when she was back to stretching barbed wire, this magical night would be nothing more than a pleasant memory.

Chapter Five

The next morning Holt was up early enough to make his rounds at the barn and get back to the house for breakfast, which Reeva normally served at five thirty.

When he entered the dining room, the dishes of food were just starting to make their way around the long oak table. The scent of warm tortillas and chorizo made his stomach growl with hunger.

Blake, who always sat at the end of the table next to their father's empty chair, looked up as Holt sat down next to his sister-in-law Roslyn.

"Good morning, Holt," he said. "I thought you were probably sleeping in."

Evelyn, his baby niece, was sitting on her mother's lap and Holt leaned over and kissed the top of her little head before he glanced down the table at Blake.

Holt smirked at him. "You know I've never slept past six o'clock in my life. Even on my sick days."

Sitting on the opposite side of Roslyn, his brother Chandler let out an amused grunt. "What sick days? You've never so much as had a sore throat."

At that moment, Jazelle leaned over Holt's shoulder to fill his cup with steaming hot coffee. He gave the maid a wink before he replied to his brother's comment.

"It's all my clean living," Holt told him. "Keeps me healthy and fit."

Everyone at the table let out good-natured groans.

"Sure, Holt," Chandler said. "If only we could all be as straitlaced as you, we'd live to be a hundred or more."

"Where's Nick and the twins?" he directed the question to his sister-in-law Katherine while he filled his plate with eggs.

"Upstairs," she told him. "The twins are still asleep and Nick volunteered to watch them while his mom has breakfast with the rest of the family."

Holt nodded knowingly. "Nick is like me. Thoughtful."

Blake and Chandler groaned. Katherine said, "Nick is thoughtful. But he's also wise. He wants to go to the res this weekend and ride horses with Hannah."

"See, the boy is like me," Holt reiterated.

Blake rolled his eyes, then asked, "So

how did your date with our new little neighbor go last night?"

Chandler glanced around the group at the table. "What new little neighbor?"

"She bought the old Landry Ranch," Blake explained. "And she's just Holt's type—young, beautiful, and single."

"What other type should I have?" Holt asked as he shook a heavy hand of black pepper over his food. "Homely and married?"

Holt had directed the question at Blake, but Chandler was the one to answer.

"I'm beginning to think you shouldn't be looking at any type," he said. "It's damned annoying to have your jilted girl-friends come into the clinic wanting me to give you nasty messages."

"Sorry," Holt told him. "The next time that happens just give her a worm pill and send her on her way."

"You're a worm all right," Blake retorted. "You worm right out of every relationship you've ever started."

Frowning, Holt picked up his coffee cup. Normally, he would simply laugh off his brothers' remarks, but this morning he wasn't feeling amused. True, after years of playing the field, he deserved a few negative comments from his family. But Blake and Chandler were already assuming that Isabelle would end up being just another jilted lover. They had no inkling that Isabelle was different. And that he had no intentions of treating her like a disposable toy.

Really, Holt? Last night when you took her home, you were practically panting for her to ask you in for a nightcap. All you could think about was creating a chance to make love to her. And if she'd given you one, you wouldn't have turned it down. So don't be thinking Isabelle is any different. That you want to be a different man with her. You can't change, Holt.

You're a cheater, a user. You'd never be able to exist as a one-woman man. So get over these soft feelings you're having toward the woman.

Hating the taunting voice in his head, Holt sipped his coffee and did his best to ignore it.

"What is this?" he asked. "Be mean to Holt morning?"

"I'm with Holt," Roslyn said. "You two are being mean to your brother. Just because you both decided to become married men doesn't mean that Holt wants to go down that same path. He has a right to date who and when he wants."

"Thank you, Ros," Holt told her. "I'm glad someone around here is willing to stand up for me. And by the way, where is Mom? She's never late to the breakfast table. Has she already eaten?"

Katherine was the one to answer. "She gulped down a cup of coffee and a doughnut. She's in a hurry to go to Phoenix this morning."

Holt exchanged a concerned look with Chandler. "Phoenix? Again?"

Chandler gave him a clueless shrug, while Blake said, "She's going to some sort of meeting for Arizona ranching women. Frankly, I think she just needs to get away for a few hours. And God knows she deserves some free time. We all know she works too hard."

A stretch of silence passed before Chandler said, "Maybe she's going to see Uncle Gil, too."

Holt stabbed his fork into the mound of eggs on his plate. For the past few months, everyone in the family had noticed a change in Maureen. At times she appeared preoccupied and even depressed. They all understood that she missed their late father. But this was something different. It was almost like she was hiding something from the family.

"Yeah. I'd make a bet she meets with Gil," Holt said flatly.

Gil was Joel's younger brother. He'd

worked on the Phoenix police force for more than thirty years and had never married. Everyone in the family had been expecting the man to soon retire, but so far he'd made no sign of giving up his career as a detective.

Holt could feel Blake's skeptical gaze boring into him.

"And what's wrong with her seeing Uncle Gil?" Blake asked. "They've always been close."

"Nothing is wrong." Holt wished he hadn't said anything. Now everyone was looking at him as though he some sort of inside information. Which he didn't.

The group around the table suddenly went silent. Except for little Evelyn. The baby began to fuss and reach her arms out for Holt to take her.

Happy for the diversion, Holt gathered the girl from Roslyn and with his arm safely around her waist, stood her on his thigh. She immediately began to laugh and tug on his ear. He tickled her belly and as she giggled with delight, Isabelle drifted through his thoughts.

I've always wanted children.

Her revelation hadn't surprised Holt. At some point in their lives, most women did want to become mothers. And yet, hearing her voice her wishes had been a reminder that she was off-limits to him. That sometime soon, he'd have to step aside and allow her to find a man who'd give her children. A man who could give her that real love she'd talked about.

For some inexplicable reason, the idea saddened him, but he wasn't going to allow himself to dwell on the situation. Isabelle was sweet and lovely and a joy to be around. It wouldn't hurt anything to date her a few more times before he told her goodbye. And by then, he was certain he'd be ready to move on to the next pretty face.

Later that afternoon, after riding fence line for more than two hours, Isabelle returned to the ranch yard and was unsaddling her horse when an old red Ford truck barreled up the long drive and pulled to a stop a few feet away from the barn.

The vehicle wasn't Holt's and Emily-Ann drove a car. Since those were the only two people she knew well enough to make the long drive out here, she couldn't imagine who this might be.

Swinging the saddle onto the top board of the corral, she walked toward the vehicle. She was halfway there when two men climbed to the ground, wearing stained straw hats, kerchiefs around their necks, and Sherpa-lined jean jackets that had seen better days.

The taller of the two lifted a hand in greeting. "Are you Ms. Townsend?"

She walked across the hard-packed dirt to join them. "I'm Isabelle Townsend," she said a bit cautiously. "This place is a far distance from town. Are you guys lost?"

"We probably look like we're lost, but

we aren't. We know this whole county like the back of our hand," the shorter one said with a wide grin. "My name is Ollie and my partner here is Sol."

Ollie had a stocky build with mousy brown hair and a mouth full of crooked teeth. His partner was as thin as a reed and what little she could see of his hair beneath the bent hat was snow-white. Isabelle gauged both men to be somewhere in their early sixties, but since the Arizona climate was rough on a person, they could've been younger.

"Nice to meet you. Is there something I can do for you?"

Sol decided it was his turn to speak. "We heard you needed ranch hands. We're here for the job."

Isabelle studied both men as her mind whirled with questions. The only people she'd talked with about hiring help was Holt, and the men who'd delivered her mares. So how did this pair know she was thinking about hiring?

"I haven't advertised for help. Who sent you here?" she asked.

Ollie cast a cagey look at his partner. "Reckon we might as well tell her, Sol. She has to know."

"Tell me what?" Isabelle asked, then decided to voice her suspicions out loud. "Did Holt Hollister send you over here?"

"Well, he didn't exactly send us," Ollie said a bit sheepishly. "It was like this, we were in the Broken Spur having a cup of coffee and he just happened to stroll in. The subject of work was brought up and he told us about you needing an honest pair of men to help you."

"And that's us, Ms. Townsend," Sol added. "Honest as the day is long. Just ask the Hollisters. We've done day work at Three Rivers for close to thirty years now."

Ollie nodded. "That's right, Ms. Townsend. And we can do about anything you might need. Sol's a damned good farrier, too. He can save you lots of money."

Isabelle didn't know what to say, much less think. These two were just the sort she needed here on the ranch. Older, polite, and experienced with ranch work. She wouldn't have to waste time showing them every little thing that needed to be done.

"You men aren't working anywhere right now?"

The two cowboys glanced at each other again as though neither one of them knew how to answer her question.

"Uh—no," Ollie told her.

Sol shook his head. "Not steady. But we can be steady for you, Ms. Townsend. We're ready to go to work right now. Got our gear in the truck."

"Well, I'm going to have to think about this," she told them. "I do need help. But there's no way I can match the wages that Three Rivers pays you. And I can only afford to use you a few hours a day. You guys are probably looking for full-time work."

Again, the two men looked at each other and Isabelle decided the pair were like twins; one didn't make a move without the other.

"Oh, no. We aren't worried about wages, Ms. Townsend," Ollie assured her. "We're happy with whatever you can pay us."

Sol added, "We're all set to work every day. We don't have anything better to do. If you got some place we can bunk, we'll be as happy as a bear in a tree full of honey."

Isabelle stared at the two men in disbelief. "I must have missed something," she said. "You two are willing to bunk here and work full-time for part-time wages?"

Sol grinned. "Why sure. That way we can sorta be your bodyguards. It's not safe for a woman like you to be living out here alone. Any kind of riffraff could wander up here at night."

Shaking her head, she said, "I don't know what to say about any of this."

"No need to say anything," Ollie told

her. "Except you might show us where we can put our saddles and our horses. We have two mares and two geldings between us. They're in the trailer waiting to be unloaded. So you won't have to worry about mounting us on working horses."

Ever since Isabelle had moved onto the ranch, she'd been worrying and wondering how she was going to hire good, reliable help. The idea that it had practically fallen into her lap had left her a little dazed and a whole lot suspicious.

"I think—" Before she could go on, the cell phone in her shirt pocket began to ring. Annoyed with the interruption, she said, "Excuse me, guys."

"You go right ahead, Ms. Townsend," Sol said. "We'll go unload our horses."

The men walked away to tend to their horses and Isabelle tugged the phone from her shirt pocket. To her surprise, the caller was Holt.

"Hello, Holt. I wasn't expecting to hear from you today."

His raspy chuckle immediately took her back to last night when he'd held her in his arms on the dance floor. She still hadn't recovered her shattered senses.

"I couldn't wait to hear your voice again," he said.

He was teasing and she took his words in that manner. "Is that why you called me? Just to hear my voice?"

He chuckled again. "Partly. I also wanted to see if Ollie and Sol have shown up yet. I thought you might be concerned and want a reference."

She looked toward the old red Ford and faded white trailer hooked behind it. The men had already unloaded one horse and Ollie was tying the bay to a hitching ring. The men were the real deal and would be a great help. But she couldn't afford them and, furthermore, Holt knew it.

"You sent them out here, didn't you?"

"They needed something to do. Presently, Three Rivers is a little crowded with help and I thought this would be a solution for all three of you."

Crowded with help? Maybe. But she had the feeling that he'd more than nudged them in her direction.

She said, "That's hard to believe. Calves start to drop in January. It's a busy time for cattle ranches."

He paused, then said, "I didn't know you knew about cattle."

"I'm hardly an expert," she admitted. "But I'm not green on the subject either. As for Ollie and Sol, they have the crazy idea that they're going to stay here on the ranch. I can't afford to pay them like round-the-clock ranch hands. I tried to make that clear to them, but they're not listening to me. I think I'd better put one of them on the phone and let you explain the situation before it gets out of hand."

"You really shouldn't concern yourself about that, Isabelle. Ollie and Sol are just happy to be helping out. They're not the type to worry about money. As long as they have a horse, a roof over their head, and something to eat, they're happy."

Isabelle was far from convinced. "What about their families? How do they support them?"

"Both men are widowers. No kids either."

The information tugged on her heartstrings. "That's sad. But it doesn't change the fact that I can only use them for three or four hours a day. Would you please make that clear to one of them?"

"Okay, put Sol on the phone. I'll set him straight."

"Thanks, Holt."

Isabelle walked over and handed the phone to Sol, then waited a few steps away while the man did more listening than talking.

Finally, Sol said, "Yeah. I understand, Holt... No. No problems here. We'll handle everything... Sure. You can count on us. I'm giving her back the phone right now."

The skinny, old cowboy handed her the phone, then without a word to her, went back to work unloading the last of the horses.

Shaking her head, Isabelle put the phone back to her ear. "Holt, I don't think you got the message across. Sol is unloading the last of the horses."

"Sol knows what he's doing. Don't argue, Isabelle. You needed good help and now you have it. Just quit asking questions and be happy."

"I am happy. But—"

"Good. Then maybe you'll invite me over soon and show me some of your cooking skills."

Totally caught off guard by the abrupt change of subject, she tried to assemble some sort of logical response. "You're asking me to cook for you?"

He chuckled. "When I say cook, I mean just give me something to eat. A sandwich will do. I'd like to come over and see the mares you shipped down from New Mexico."

Last night, when he'd brought her home, she'd very nearly made the mistake of asking him in for coffee. A part of her hadn't wanted the time with him to end. But thankfully, common sense had won over and instead of inviting him in, she'd given him a quick kiss on the cheek and rushed into the house.

"Isabelle, are you still there?"

She mentally shook herself. "Uh—yes, I was just thinking. It's foaling season. Aren't you terribly busy right now?"

"I figure I'll have a few days of peace until the next moon change. It comes on Monday. What are you doing tomorrow night?"

"Aren't you being a bit pushy? We just went out last night."

"And it was very nice, wasn't it?"

Too nice, Isabelle thought. Now every little nuance about the man seemed stuck in her head.

"Yes," she agreed. "It was enjoyable."

"Then why shouldn't we see each other again?"

Isabelle was smart enough to recognize that if she continued to see the man, she'd soon wind up in bed with him. And no matter how sexy or pleasant his company was, an affair with a playboy wouldn't be a smart choice. Now or ever.

And yet, she was starting a new life here in Yavapai County. It was nice and helpful to have a fellow horse trainer to talk with.

"No reason," she answered, then before she could change her mind added impishly, "I suppose I could manage to put some cold cuts between two slices of bread. Would that be enough cooking for you?"

He chuckled. "Sounds perfect. I'll be there before dark."

"I'll see you then."

Not giving him time to say more, she ended the call and dropped the phone back into her pocket. Tomorrow would be soon enough to worry about having Holt over for dinner. Right now she had to make two old ranch hands understand she couldn't use them on a full-time basis.

The next afternoon, after finishing several chores in Wickenburg, Isabelle decided to treat herself to a short break. When she dropped by Conchita's coffee shop for an espresso and frosted doughnut, Emily-Ann greeted her with a huge hug.

"If you hadn't shown up soon, I was going to file a missing person report," Emily-Ann said as the two women sat outside at one of the little wrought iron tables. "I haven't seen or heard from you since the morning you went to Three Rivers and had it out with Holt."

Isabelle carefully sipped the hot espresso, then lowered the cup back to the table. "The next day I went back to Three Rivers and things went far better with Holt. I ended up buying five mares from him."

Emily-Ann smiled brightly and Isabelle decided the young woman looked extra pretty today wearing a canary yellow sweater with her red hair braided over one shoulder.

"Now that's more like it," she said with approval. "I was going to be truly surprised if he didn't come through with a good deal for you."

"The mares are exceptional. Their babies should fetch a good price," Isabelle told her. "I'm thrilled to get them."

Emily-Ann leaned eagerly toward her. "Forget the horses. I want to hear how you got on with Holt? You were mighty angry with him."

Isabelle could feel her cheeks growing warm. "We, uh, got on fine. Actually, we went on a date—to dinner."

Emily-Ann's mouth fell open. "You're kidding, right?"

"It was against my better judgment, but

I did go," Isabelle admitted. "And frankly, I had a lovely time. It was nice to be out and away from all the work on the ranch for a few hours."

"Wowee!" Emily-Ann exclaimed. "You actually went on a date with Holt! I'm stunned. Not that Holt asked you out. But that you agreed to go!"

Isabelle shrugged. "I couldn't very well refuse. From what he told me, he had no intentions of selling any more mares this year. I was fortunate that he agreed to part with those five. The least I could do was show him my appreciation."

Emily-Ann giggled. "Sure, Isabelle."

Frowning, Isabelle picked up her espresso. "You act as though he's some sort of rock star in a cowboy hat."

Emily-Ann shrugged. "I admit I sound silly. But he's one of the most eligible bachelors around here. Doesn't it make you feel special that he's interested—in you? It would me. But then nobody of his caliber is ever going to take a second glance at me."

The frown on Isabelle's face deepened. "This isn't the first time I've heard you putting yourself down, Emily-Ann, and I want you to stop it. You're a bright, lovely woman. You're just as good as me or Holt or any person."

She smiled wanly. "If you say so."

"I do say so." Isabelle popped the last of the doughnut into her mouth and savored the taste before she swallowed it down. "I've got to be going. I have the truck loaded down with groceries. Oh, I almost forgot—I have two hired hands now. Ollie Sanders and Sol Reynolds. Do you know them?"

Emily-Ann shook her head. "I'm not familiar with either name, but I might recognize them if I saw them. Are they the sort to stop by here for coffee?"

Isabelle laughed at the image. "No. This pair is a little rough around the edges for Conchita's."

Bemused, Emily-Ann gestured to the small building behind them and the simple outdoor tables. "This place is hardly fancy. What kind of guys are they?"

"The sort that drink plain coffee at the Broken Spur. Ollie's sixty-one and Sol is sixty-three. Neither has a family and ranch work is the only job they've ever had."

Emily-Ann frowned. "Are you sure you can trust these guys? Where did you find them anyway?"

"Holt sent them over. They normally work at Three Rivers. Now they're staying on Blue Stallion with me. I'm helping them turn one of the feed rooms into a little bunkhouse so they'll have a comfortable place to stay. I already had a hot plate for them to use and today I bought a small fridge. Next I need to purchase a couple of single beds and some linen. Last night they slept on cots and sleeping bags."

Emily-Ann frowned thoughtfully. "Are

you sure these guys are going to be worth the extra money they're costing you?"

Isabelle nodded. "They've already done more in one day than I could do in ten. And don't get the idea that they're too old to be useful. Both of them could work circles around a man in his thirties."

"Sounds like you're happy with these guys," Emily-Ann remarked.

"I couldn't be more pleased," Isabelle told her. "But there is something nagging at me. When I told them the amount I'd be able to pay for a monthly wage, I expected them to turn tail and leave. Instead they seemed indifferent. It's weird."

Emily-Ann drummed her fingers thoughtfully against the tabletop. "Interesting that Holt sent them over. If I didn't know better, it sounds like he's trying to take care of you."

Isabelle reacted with a sound that was something between a grunt and a laugh. "That's ridiculous. Holt is only being a helpful neighbor."

The smirk on her Emily-Ann's lips said exactly what she thought about Isabelle's explanation. "None of my neighbors have ever been *that* helpful."

Isabelle didn't want to get annoyed with Emily-Ann. She was the closest friend she had here in Wickenburg and she genuinely liked her. Even though she did get these silly notions.

"Look, Emily-Ann, I'm sure you'd be the first person to advise me against getting serious about Holt Hollister," Isabelle told her. "So let me assure you. He's a friend and that's all he'll ever be to me."

Emily-Ann rolled her eyes. "How funny, Isabelle. Me giving you advice about a man. But I happen to think it would be fitting if you'd give Mr. Holt Hollister some of the same love 'em and leave 'em medicine he's dished out over the years."

Isabelle crumpled the wax paper that her doughnut had been wrapped in and dropped it in her empty cup. Thank goodness she hadn't mentioned to Emily-Ann that Holt was coming over to the ranch this evening. She'd really be having a field day with that tidbit of information.

"I thought he was an old family friend of yours," Isabelle remarked.

"He is. But it's past time he met his match." She smiled cleverly. "And I happen to think you're it."

"Oh, no. Not me." Isabelle rose to her feet just as a customer pulled into the parking area of the coffee shop. "Time for me to go. See you, Emily-Ann."

Emily-Ann waggled her fingers. "Drop by soon. I can't wait to hear what you'll have to tell me then."

Rolling her eyes, Isabelle pulled the strap of her purse onto her shoulder. "The next time I stop by for coffee, you're not going to hear one thing about Holt Hollister. And that's a promise."

Emily-Ann laughed. "You know what they say about promises. They're made to be broken."

Chapter Six

Sundown was still more than an hour away when Holt arrived on Blue Stallion Ranch. As he parked the truck a short distance from the house and climbed to the ground, he noticed a cloud of brown dust rising near the barn area.

Squinting against the lingering rays of sunlight, Holt spotted Isabelle in a large round pen riding a little bay mare with a white blaze down her face. Ollie and Sol were perched on a rail of the fence, watching their new boss in action.

As Holt approached the two men, Ollie threw up a hand in greeting. "Hey, Holt. Come have a seat and watch the show. Isabelle's got the little mare spinning on a dime."

Holt leaned a shoulder against the fence and peered through the wooden rails as Isabelle continued to put the mare through a series of maneuvers.

Sol said, "I never thought I'd see anyone ride as well as you, Holt, but Isabelle comes pretty damned close."

Holt glanced up at the older man. "Aww, come on, now, Sol," he joked. "You think that just because she's a lot prettier than me."

Ollie chuckled. "Well, I wouldn't argue that point. But she sure knows how to handle horses. Surprised the heck out of me and Sol, that's for sure."

Holt turned his attention back to the pen just in time to see Isabelle rein the mare to a skidding stop. He couldn't argue that she sat the saddle in fine form. Loose and relaxed while being in total control, it was easy to see she was a very experienced rider. She was also the sexiest thing that Holt had ever laid eyes on.

Maybe that was why he couldn't stay away from the woman, he silently reasoned. It wasn't like him to take time away from the ranch when foals were coming right and left. But this evening when he'd made his rounds through the barns, the mares he'd put on foal watch had all seemed settled and happy. And if by chance one did decide to suddenly go into labor, Holt knew he could depend on T.J. and Chandler to handle the situation.

For the past few years, Holt's family had been urging him to ease his workload and spend more time away from the horse barn. Preferably finding himself a good wife and growing a family. Hell, why would he want to fence himself in like that? Even with a woman like Isabelle.

He was pushing the question aside when

she suddenly spotted him and trotted the mare over to where he was standing near the fence.

"Hi, Holt. I wasn't expecting you this early," she said with an easy smile. "I haven't made those sandwiches I promised you yet."

He smiled back at her and wondered why seeing her made him feel like he was standing on a golden cloud with bright blue sky all around him.

"I'm not worried. I doubt you're going to let me starve."

Isabelle dismounted and led the mare out of a gate and around the fence to where Holt was standing.

Before she reached him, Ollie and Sol climbed to the ground and she handed the sweaty mare over to the two men.

"We'll take care of her," Ollie told Isabelle. "You go on with your visit."

"Thank you, guys."

The two men left with the horse in tow and Holt turned his attention to Isabelle.

Her perfect little curves were covered with a pair of faded jeans and a yellow-and-brown-striped shirt. A dark brown cowboy hat covered her white-blond hair, while spurs jingled on the heels of her boots.

To him, she looked just as pretty in her work clothes as she had in the clingy black dress she'd worn to dinner, and Holt decided just looking at her made him feel happier than he'd felt in years.

"I noticed you didn't give the men any instructions about the mare," he said.

She shook her head. "I don't have to tell them anything. They know exactly what to do. But you knew that when you sent them over here."

So she'd figured that out. "Aren't you glad I did?"

She pondered his question for only a second. "I'm very glad. And if I haven't said thank you, I'm saying it now."

"No thanks needed," he replied, while telling himself there was no need for her to ever find out the whole deal about Ollie and Sol. Sure, he'd sent them over here, and that was all she needed to know.

She swiped the back of her sleeve against her cheeks and said, "Sorry I look such a mess. We've been repairing a bunch of feed troughs this afternoon and then I decided to give Pin-Up Girl a little exercise."

"No need to apologize. You look as pretty as Pin-Up Girl," he said.

She laughed and he realized he liked that about her, too. That she could laugh at him and herself.

"Thank you, Holt. Before we head to the house, would you like to walk on down to the barn and take a look at my horses?"

"I would like that," he told her. "And by the way, your little Pin-Up Girl looks great. Did you train her?"

She stepped up to his side and as they began to amble in the direction of the big weathered barn, Holt had to fight the urge to curl his arm around the back of her waist.

"Thank you. Yes, I did train her," she answered. "She's only three. She was born to one of my mares shortly after I moved to Albuquerque. It's only been these past few months that I've had a chance to work with her on a regular basis."

Albuquerque. He was beginning to hate the mention of that city. Not that he had anything against it. But he did resent the reminder of her ex and the married life she'd had with the man. Which was stupid of him, Holt realized. He'd dated divorced women before and nothing about their exes had bothered him in the least. He had no right or reason to be jealous or possessive of Isabelle.

"I'll be honest," he said, "When I saw you that first day you came to Three Rivers, I thought—"

Intrigued, she prodded, "You thought what?"

Right now he figured he looked as sheepish as the day Reeva had caught him digging into a pie she'd made especially for his sister Vivian's birthday party. Thankfully his sister had always forgiven him anything. He wasn't sure that Isabelle would be so forgiving, though.

He said, "That you looked like you spent most of your time on a tropical beach. That you were probably one of those women who wanted to try a new hobby every few months. And this month just happened to be horses."

Her laugh was deep and genuine. "What a wonderful impression you had of me. Is that why you gave me the cold shoulder?"

What was wrong with him? Nothing embarrassed him, or so he thought. But now that he was beginning to know Isabelle, he wanted her to think highly of him.

"I'm sorry about that, Isabelle. I was being a real ass that morning. But you see, I have a problem with women."

"Yes, I've heard that."

Her deadpan response had him laughing. "I'm sure you've heard plenty of things. What I meant was I have problems with women showing up at the barn as though it's a petting zoo. Most of them don't understand that horses can be very dangerous. Especially to a greenhorn. Then there's the loss of time and work it takes for one of the hands to escort the woman around the barn. It's worse than annoying. It's like I said—a problem."

"I see. You thought the only kind of horse I'd ever ridden was the kind where you drop a quarter in the slot." Her smile was playful. "I forgive you. After all, you'd never met me. But that should teach you not to make assumptions just by appearances."

"That's a lesson our mother tried to drive in all of us kids. I guess it didn't stick with me."

She chuckled. "Well, I wouldn't worry, Holt. You're still very young. You have plenty of time to learn."

* * *

Shadows were stretching across the ranch yard and the warmth of the spring-like day had begun to cool when Isabelle and Holt finally walked to the house.

"I do hope you're hungry," Isabelle told him as they entered a door on the back porch. "I have a surprise for you."

He followed her into the kitchen. "Let me guess. You got more than one kind of lunch meat. Bologna, I hope. That's my favorite."

"I do have bologna. But I—"

She paused as she turned to see him sniffing the air.

"Something is cooking and it doesn't smell like sandwiches."

She walked over to a large gas range and switched off the oven. "No. I decided to take pity on you and give you something besides bread and cold cuts. But don't get too excited until you do a taste test. This dish is one of the few things I can cook and it doesn't always turn out right. If we dig in and it tastes awful, I'll drag out the bologna."

"With an offer like that, I can't lose." He held up his hands. "If you'll show me where I can wash up, I'll help you get things ready."

"Follow me. The bathroom is just down the hall," she told him.

They left the kitchen and started down a narrow hallway. Isabelle could feel his presence following close behind her and she wondered what would happen if she suddenly stopped and turned to face him? Would he want to kiss her? Had the thought of kissing her ever crossed his mind?

Stop it, Isabelle! You're a fool for thinking about such things! You just got out of a loveless marriage. Why would you want to enter into a loveless affair? Just so you could feel a man's strong arms around you? Forget it.

Shutting her mind off to the silent warning, she hurried ahead of him and opened the bathroom door. "Here it is," she said. "Help yourself and I'll, uh, see you back in the kitchen."

"Thanks."

As soon as he disappeared into the bathroom, Isabelle rushed to her bedroom and threw off her hat. After dashing a hairbrush through her hair, she swiped on pink lipstick, sighed helplessly at the dusty image in the mirror, and hurried back to the kitchen.

She'd barely had time to take the casserole out of the oven when Holt returned to the room and sidled up to her at the gas range.

"That really smells good, Isabelle," he said. "But you've made me feel awful. I honestly didn't expect you to cook."

There were plenty of things about Holt that Isabelle hadn't expected, she thought. After their dinner date a couple of nights ago, she hadn't figured on seeing him again. At least, not this soon or in such an intimate setting. And from all she'd heard about his womanizing, she'd expected him to be making all kinds of sexual advances. So far she'd been all wrong about the man.

She cast him a droll look. "That is what you suggested on the phone."

"Yes, but I was only using that as an excuse to invite myself over."

She couldn't stop a playful smile from tugging at her lips. "I know that."

He grinned. "And you cooked for me anyway. That's sweet, Isabelle."

His eyes were twinkling as a grin spread slowly across his face. The tempting sight jumped her heart into overdrive and she knew if she didn't move away from him, she was going to say or do something stupid. Like rest her palm against his chest and tilt her lips toward his.

Drawing in a shaky breath, she turned and moved down the cabinets to where the dishes were stored.

"Just don't let it go to your head," she said. "And if you want to make yourself useful, you might fill some glasses with ice while I set the table."

"Ice? No wine?"

"Sorry. I'm out of wine. I have tea, soda, or water."

"I should've brought a bottle, but I thought we were having sandwiches. Water is plenty fine for me, though." He found the glasses and was filling them with crushed ice when he suddenly snapped his fingers. "Oh, I nearly forgot! I have something for us in the truck. I'll be right back."

He hurried out the back door of the kitchen and while he was gone, Isabelle set the table in the dining room, then added the food and drinks. She was lighting a tall yellow candle when he walked in carrying a round plastic container.

"This is nice, Isabelle." Standing next to her, he slowly surveyed the long room. "I love all the arched windows. You can see all the way to the barn from here."

"Yes and the mountains beyond. This is

one of my favorite rooms in the house." She gestured behind them to the table and matching china hutch. "One of these days, I'm going to get more furniture. Like a longer dining table and a buffet to go with it. But since it's just me and I don't do any entertaining, there isn't much need for me to rush into furniture shopping. Actually, if you weren't here tonight, I'd be eating in the kitchen."

"Nothing wrong with that. I do it quite often because I'm usually late coming in from the barn. And sometimes I just want to have Reeva for company."

She pointed to the plastic container he was holding. "Is that something to eat?"

He grinned. "Pie. Blueberry with double crust. I asked Reeva to make it especially for us. I hope you like blueberries."

"I love them and what a treat to have a homemade pie." Isabelle took the container from him and set it on the table alongside the casserole, then motioned for him to take a seat. "Everything is ready. Let's eat."

"Not until the hostess is seated." He pulled out her chair and made a sweeping gesture with his arm. "For you, my lady."

She laughed softly. "What am I? Cinderella in dusty blue jeans?"

"Of course you are. And I'm the prince in cowboy boots. But I wasn't thinking. I should've brought you a glass slipper instead of a blueberry pie."

He pushed her and the chair forward and once she was comfortably positioned, she expected him to move on around to the other side of the table. Instead, he lingered there with his hands on the back of the chair and Isabelle held her breath, waiting and wondering if his hands were going to slide onto her shoulders.

But they didn't and when he finally stepped away, she expelled a breath of relief. Or was that disappointment she was feeling? Oh, Lord, the man shook her like nothing ever had. And he'd not so much as kissed her or even touched her in a romantic way. She must be losing her grip, she thought.

"No need to worry," she said. "I threw the other glass slipper away a long time ago."

He took the seat across from her, then leaned his forearms against the edge of the table and looked at her. "I think you meant that as a joke, but you didn't exactly sound like you were teasing."

"If I sounded cynical, I didn't mean to," she said. "It's just that sometimes I get to thinking about—" She paused and shook her head. "You don't want to hear this kind of stuff. Let's eat. You go first."

She picked up a large serving spoon and handed it to him.

He filled his plate with a large portion of the Mexican-type casserole, then reached for a basket of tortilla chips. "I do want to hear. What is it that puts you in a pessimistic mood?"

She shrugged, while wishing she'd

never said anything. "Okay, I get to thinking about all the time I wasted trying to make things be the way I wanted them to be."

He frowned. "You're very young, Isabelle. You have plenty of time to make your life's dreams come true."

Dreams. Yes, she'd always had those. But only one of them was coming true. Her dream of Blue Stallion Ranch. And that's the one she needed to focus on. Not on a man to hold her tight or put a ring on her finger or give her children.

She gave him the cheeriest smile she could muster and began to fill her plate. "You're right, Holt. I have my whole life ahead of me. I might just go buy myself a new pair of glass slippers and kick up my heels."

"Now that's more like it."

He reached across the table for her hand and as his fingers wrapped warmly around hers, she arched a questioning brow at him.

"What's wrong?" she asked impishly. "You think I'm going to run away from the table and leave you with all the mess?"

His thumb gently rubbed the back of her hand. The soft touch caused a layer of goose bumps to cover her arms. Thankfully, with her arms hidden by long sleeves, he couldn't see just how much he was affecting her.

"No. I was just thinking how pretty you look and how much I'm enjoying being here with you like this."

Her cheeks grew warm and she figured they had turned a telltale pink. "You're flirting now," she murmured accusingly.

"A little," he admitted. "But I'm also telling the truth. You can't know what it's like being in a big family with three-fourths of us living under the same roof. It can get loud. And it takes work to find any sort of privacy."

Before she melted right there in her chair, she eased her hand from his and picked up her fork. "But it must be nice having brothers and sisters. I've always thought having siblings would be wonderful."

"It is. And I'm very close to all of them. It's just that sometimes I want to be alone and keep my thoughts to myself."

She nodded, then smiled. "Or perhaps just talk to the cook."

"Yes, thank God for Reeva. I can say what I really think to her. She gets me. How she does, I don't know. The woman is seventy-one. Nearly forty years older than me."

He took a bite of the food and Isabelle could tell from the look on his face that he liked it. The fact sent a ridiculous spurt of joy through her.

"Age isn't what makes two people click. It's being on the same plane and having the right chemistry mix and a lot of other things."

He looked up from his plate and Isabelle felt a jolt as his gaze met hers.

"You sound like my sister Viv. She's always telling me that one of these days I'll find a woman who I'll click with. One I'll want to be with the rest of my life."

"And what do you say to her?"

"I mostly laugh."

"Why? Because you want to change women like you change shirts?"

"Ouch! If that's how you think of me, then why did you invite me here tonight?"

That was a good question, Isabelle thought. Just why exactly was she spending time with Holt when she knew there was no future in it?

"You invited yourself, remember? And I agreed to it."

"Because?"

The smile she gave him came from deep inside her. "I like you, Holt. And I like your company. And I'm not expecting anything more from you than friendship. That's why I agreed to see you again."

He studied her face for long moments and Isabelle was struck by the look in his eyes. It was almost like she was seeing hurt or disappointment, yet that couldn't be right, she thought. Holt was a guy who was just out for a good time. He wasn't wanting anything from her, unless it was sex. And so far, he'd not given her any sign that he wanted even that.

"Hmm. That's fair enough. And being your friend would be special for me. I've never had a female friend before."

No, she thought dismally, he most likely considered them lovers rather than friends. "You have Reeva," she told him.

"She's like a second mom."

"What about Jazelle? The blond woman who brought the pastries to your office?"

He nodded. "Jazelle is like family, too. She's been with us for a long time."

"Really? She looks very young."

He ate a few bites of the casserole before he commented. "She is. But she came to work for us when she was only in her teens, so we've all known her for a long time. She's a single mother of a little boy. He's probably four or five now. Sometimes she brings him out to the ranch, but mostly her mother watches him while Jazelle works."

A single mother. Isabelle hadn't ended up being one of those, but sometimes she wished Trevor had given her a child. Even though he hadn't loved her, a child would've been something more than his money could buy. With a child, she wouldn't be so alone now. She'd have a real purpose and reason to build her ranch. And most of all, she'd have someone to give her love to. But he'd kept putting her desire to have a baby on the something-to-do-later list, like many years later.

Shoving those miserable thoughts aside, she asked, "What about your siblings? Do they have children?"

He laughed. "Lots of them. Blake and Kat have a son, Nick. He's getting close to thirteen. And then they have twin toddlers, Abagail and Andrew. Chandler and his wife, Roslyn, have a baby girl, Evelyn. Viv has a fourteen-year-old daughter,

Hannah, and she recently learned the baby she's carrying is actually twins. Joseph, my youngest brother, has a three-year-old boy, Little Joe, and they're expecting again, too."

"Sounds like the Hollister family is growing fast. So you're the only one who isn't married with children?"

"No. My baby sister, Camille, is still single. She lives at our other ranch, Red Bluff. And before you ask," he added with a little laugh, "none of the horses down there are for sale."

She laughed with him. "Well, it never hurts to try."

When Holt finally pushed his plate to one side, the casserole dish was nearly empty and the corn chips were little more than a pile of crumbs in the bottom of the basket.

"You were telling a fib when you said you couldn't cook, Isabelle. That was delicious."

"Thanks, I'm glad you liked it." She stood and began to gather dishes. "Don't forget we have Reeva's pie for dessert. I'll carry these things to the kitchen and get some coffee going."

"I'll help you." Rising from the chair, he collected his dirty plate and silverware and followed her out of the dining room.

"Actually, there's something other than the dishes that you could help me with," she said. "Do you know how to build a fire?"

His gaze instinctively dropped to the sway of her shapely little butt. "What kind of fire are you talking about?"

Glancing over her shoulder, she pulled a playful face at him. "I'm not asking you to be an arsonist, if that's what you're thinking. I'm talking about the fireplace."

He'd forgotten she even had a fireplace. His mind was too preoccupied with the bedroom. Damn it! He must be developing some sort of personality disorder. What else would explain his uncharacteristic behavior? Where women were concerned, he'd always had one objective. Until the morning Isabelle sat in his office looking like a breath of spring. From that day on, something had tilted in his head. Now he wanted Isabelle more than any woman he'd ever known, but he was hesitant to even allow himself to touch her. What the heck was he doing here anyway?

Seeing that she'd paused to look at him, he mentally shook himself and tried to sound normal. "The fireplace," he repeated inanely. "Sure, I'm great at building fires."

The faint curve of her lips told Holt she'd also been thinking about another kind of fire. The notion not only surprised him, it rattled him right down to his boots. Making love to Isabelle might prove to be fatal to his common sense. That was something he needed to remember.

"I thought you would be."

Holt kept his mouth shut as he followed

her into the kitchen and, after depositing the dishes in the sink, he went to deal with the fire.

In the living room, he found wood and kindling stacked on the left side of the fireplace and matches lying near a poker stand. In a few short minutes, he was standing with his back to the flames, soaking up the heat while he waited for Isabelle to appear.

When she finally entered the room, carrying a tray with the pie and coffee, she glanced appreciatively at the blazing fire.

"That's nice, Holt." She walked over and placed the tray on the coffee table in front of the couch. "I can feel the heat all the way over here."

So could he, Holt thought, and it had nothing to do with the burning mesquite logs.

"Come on over," she invited as she took a seat on the long green couch.

Holt left the fireplace to join her and took a seat more than two feet away from her, all the while his brothers' mocking laughter sounded in his ears. If they could see him now, they'd never believe it, he thought wryly.

"Help yourself, Holt," she said. "I brought the whole pie so that you could cut the size you want."

"I'll do yours first," he told her.

After he handed her a dish of the pie and cut a hefty portion for himself, she said, "If you like, I can turn on the TV. I have satellite so the reception is good and there's plenty of channels to choose from."

"I don't necessarily need it, unless you'd like to watch." He settled back with the desert and tried to forget that the two of them were alone. That fire was warm and she'd be even warmer in his arms.

"It must be a horse trainer thing," she commented between bites of pie. "I don't watch either. After a day in the saddle, I don't have the time or desire to watch."

"Once I grew past cartoon age, I forgot all about TV."

She slanted an amused glance at him and he chuckled.

"What's wrong?" he asked. "You can't imagine me watching Looney Tunes?"

"I can see you rooting for that nasty coyote," she teased. "He's just your type. Fast and wily."

"I'll tell you one thing, I can't see you as the little helpless heroine tied to the railroad track yelling for help," he replied, then arched a questioning brow in her direction. "Do you ever yell for help?"

"Things have to get pretty desperate before I yell," she admitted. "But we all need a helping hand sometimes. And being too proud to accept it is really stupid."

And she was far from stupid, Holt thought. In fact, he'd never dated any woman who was ambitious and hard-working enough to build a ranch on her own. Was that why he was feeling so different about Isabelle? Because he admired and respected all those things about her? He wished he knew the answers. Maybe then he wouldn't be feeling like he'd lost all control of his faculties.

"I'm glad you accepted Ollie's and Sol's help," he said. "I won't be worrying about you so much."

She frowned and reached for her coffee. "Worrying about me? You shouldn't be doing that."

She was right. He had no right or reason to be fretting about her well-being. But something about Isabelle brought out the protector in him.

"Anything could happen to you out here. If a horse bucked you off and the fall broke your leg—" He paused and shook his head. "Well, it's just better that the men are here with you."

A gentle smile crossed her face and Holt noticed that even with her lipstick gone, her lips were still a soft pink. The color reminded him of cotton candy and he figured she'd taste just as sweet as the delicate treat.

"I'm glad the men are here, too," she said. "I like their company. I'm learning Ollie is the more talkative of the two and can be very funny at times. Sol is more solemn and serious, but just as nice."

She leaned forward to place her cup on the coffee table and Holt watched her silky hair slide forward to drape against her cheek. He didn't have to be told the color was natural. The texture was too smooth and the shades too varied to be anything but what she'd been born with. Which made the pale color even more amazing.

He was fighting the urge to reach out and touch the strands when she suddenly took away the opportunity by straightening from the coffee table and settling back in her seat.

A pent-up breath rushed out of him and he quickly decided he needed to leave before he lost control and allowed himself to do something that might ruin their relationship.

Relationship, hell! What are you thinking, Holt? You don't have any kind of connection to this woman! And even if you did, what good would it do? The Holt Hollister you once were is gone. He's turned into some sort of mushy cream puff. Since when did you ever worry about pulling a woman into your arms and kissing her?

Since he'd met Isabelle, that's when, he silently shouted back at the cynical voice revolving around in his head.

Suddenly feeling trapped, he started to rise and cross to the fireplace. At the same time she chose that moment to shift around on the couch so that she was facing him and Holt stayed where he was.

She asked, "Have you ever had any serious horse injuries?"

Grateful for the momentary distraction, he scooped up the last of his pie and placed the small dessert plate onto the coffee table.

"If I start listing all my injuries, you're going to think I'd be lucky to ride a tricycle."

She laughed. "Not hardly. I've taken plenty of spills and bites and kicks. It just goes with the job."

He nodded. "I've had black eyes and a lost tooth. A broken ankle that required surgery to repair. A cracked wrist and ribs. Oh, yeah, and a dislocated shoulder. I've had a few concussions, too. Which my siblings say I've never fully recovered from."

"That's mean of them."

"They like to tease me."

Her gaze dropped away from his. "I do, too," she murmured. "I like how you're such a good sport about it."

His mocking conscience had been wrong, Holt thought ruefully. He wasn't even a cream puff anymore. She'd just turned him into a melted marshmallow.

"Is that all you like—about me?" he asked.

She looked up at him and Holt was fascinated with the way the corners of her lips tilted upward.

"I like that you laugh about certain things instead of whine and complain."

There she went again, touching a spot in him that he'd thought was long dead. "Dad always taught his sons that real men don't whine, they fix."

"Sounds like your father was a wise and fair man," she said.

"He was all that and more. It's no wonder that Mom—" He broke off, surprised that he'd been about to share more personal details about his family with her. He didn't do that with other women. Why did it just automatically seem to come out when he was with Isabelle? "Right now she's going through a rough patch emotionally."

"We all go through those." Her gaze slid earnestly over his face. "Are you worried about her?"

She wasn't just mouthing a question.

She really cared, he thought. The idea pierced something deep inside his chest.

"No," he said, then shrugged. "Well, perhaps a little. But she's a trouper. Eventually she'll get smoothed out. I'm sure of that."

She nodded and Holt told himself it was beyond time for him to go home. Even if the evening was still early, he was asking for trouble to keep staying.

He was about to push himself up from the couch and announce he was leaving, but then he heard her sigh. The sound prompted him to look at her and all at once his intentions of fleeing were forgotten.

"The fire is so lovely," she murmured. "It's especially nice when it's quiet like this and you can hear the logs crackling."

What he found lovely was the way the glow of the flames was turning her smooth skin to a pale gold and lit her blue eyes with soft yellow lights.

"Do you ever get lonely here, Isabelle?"

Her head turned toward his and his heart skipped a beat as he watched her lips slowly spread into a smile.

"I'm not lonely now. You're here," she said simply.

Something in him snapped and before he could stop himself, he was sliding over to her and wrapping his hands over the tops of shoulders.

"Isabelle, I—" He paused unsure of what he wanted or needed to say.

When he failed to go on, she shook her head. "I thought you didn't want me—like this. Do you?"

The doubt in her voice was so opposite of the yearning inside him that he groaned with frustration. "You can't imagine how much I want you, Isabelle. How much I want to do this."

He didn't give her, or himself, time to think about anything. He lowered his head until their foreheads were touching and his lips were lightly brushing against hers. She tasted soft and sweet and as tantalizing as a hot drink on a frigid night.

"I've thought too much about you," she whispered. "About how much I wanted this to happen."

Her last words tore away the safety he'd tried to erect between them and the next thing he knew, his lips were moving over hers like a thirsty man who'd finally found an oasis.

This wasn't a kiss, he thought. It was a wild collision. A wreck of his senses.

After a few seconds, he recognized he was in deep trouble. He needed to put on the brakes and lever some space between them before he lost all control. But how was he supposed to stop something that felt so incredibly good? Why would he ever want to end this delicious connection? He'd never felt so thrilled, or had so many emotions humming through his veins.

Her arms slipped around his neck and then the front of her body was pressing tightly against his. Desire exploded in his head and shot a burning arrow straight to his loins.

The assault on his senses very nearly paralyzed him and even though he was silently shouting at himself to pull back, he did just the opposite and deepened the kiss.

It wasn't until she broke the contact of their lips and began to press tiny kisses along his jaw that a scrap of sanity hit his brain.

"Isabelle, this isn't good," he whispered, then groaned. "I mean—it is good—so good, but not the, uh, right thing for us."

That was enough to snap her head back and she stared at him in dazed wonder. "Oh. I—thought. I don't understand, Holt."

"Neither do I," he said gruffly, then quickly jumped to his feet before he had the chance to change his mind and pull her back into his arms. "I really like you,

Isabelle. I like you too much for this. So I—have to leave. Now."

He turned and hurried out to the kitchen to collect his hat from the end of the cabinet. By the time he'd skewered it onto his head and reached the back door, Isabelle had caught up to him.

"You're leaving now?"

The confusion in her voice intensified his determination to keep a space of sanity between them.

"Yes. I'm sorry, Isabelle. But I—don't want to ruin things with us."

She marched over to where he stood with his hand already clutching the doorknob.

"Ruin things? How do you mean? You kissed me and realized you didn't like it? Well, all you have to do is tell me so, Holt. You don't have to hightail it out of here to avoid being tortured again!"

Tortured? Yes, that was the perfect word for it, Holt thought. But not in the way she'd meant.

Spurred by her ridiculous remark, he snatched a hold on her upper arm and tugged her forward. She stumbled awkwardly against him and Holt was quick to take advantage by once again latching his lips over hers.

This time the kiss was just as deep, but he managed to end it before it turned into something neither of them was ready for.

"Good night, Isabelle. And thanks for the dinner."

She didn't reply. Or if she did, Holt didn't stay around to hear it. He left the house and hurried to his truck before he lost the last shred of decency he possessed. Before she had a chance to see the real Holt Hollister. The one who gobbled up sweet little things like her and moved on to the next one.

Chapter Seven

Two days later, Holt entered Blake's office, located at the north end of the main cattle barn. A few years ago, his older brother had worked out of the study where their father had always dealt with all the ranch's official business. But as Three Rivers had continued to grow, Blake and the rest of the family had agreed it would be best to have the flow of ranch clients away from the house.

With Holt's office still a cubbyhole that had once been a tack room, he often teased his older brother about having the fancy digs to work in, while he had to deal with barn dust and pack rats. But in truth, Blake deserved the comfortable office, along with a devoted secretary, who helped him carry the heavy load of managing Three Rivers Ranch.

"Good morning, Flo," he said to the older woman sitting behind a large cherry wood desk.

She peered at him over the tops of her bifocals and as Holt took in her short red hair and matching lipstick, he figured in her younger years she'd been a raving beauty. Now, toward the end of her sixties, she was sporting some wrinkles. But there was still a shrewd gleam in her brown eyes that told Holt she'd dealt with men like him before and had always come out the winner.

"Morning, Holt. You have work for me today?"

There were times when he got behind

on his paperwork and Flo was always charitable enough to do it for him.

"No. I'll need some registrations done on the new babies soon, but that can wait. I need to talk with Blake for a few minutes."

She jerked her thumb toward the closed door to Blake's portion of the office. "He's in there and your mother is with him."

"Good. I'll hit her up to give you a raise. You deserve one for putting up with Blake, don't you?"

"Ha!" She snorted. "I deserve a huge one for putting up with you."

Laughing, he patted the secretary's cheek before he crossed the room and entered Blake's office.

"What's going on in here? A family powwow?" He walked over to where his mother was standing at the window and smacked a kiss on her cheek. "Hi, Mom. You look beautiful this morning."

She wrapped her arm around his waist and gave him a little hug. "Okay, what are you wanting? Blake has already told you we're not getting an equine pool. At least, not yet."

"I'm not worried about a pool. But just think what a great tax write-off it would be," he said, slanting a pointed look at Blake, who was sitting casually at his desk. "Probably save the ranch a few thousand."

"We need another well drilled if we're going to turn that range over by Juniper Ridge into a hay meadow. And you know that isn't going to come cheap."

"Maybe we ought to just get more hay shipped in," Holt suggested. "The Timothy/alfalfa mix we get from Nevada is great."

"And very expensive." Maureen spoke up. "We have the climate and the machinery to grow and bale our own. All we need is water and it isn't going to fall from the sky, unfortunately."

"Sometimes it does. If you'd open those

blinds and look outside right now, you might see otherwise," Holt told her.

She peeked through the slatted blinds and gasped. "It is raining! Oh, and I left my horse hitched in the arena and he's wearing my favorite saddle! I'd better run!"

Maureen raced out of the office and Holt walked over and sank into the chair in front of Blake's desk. "The rain started about ten minutes ago. Mom's saddle is probably already soaked."

"Some of the hands will oil it for her," Blake said, then leaning back in his chair, he crossed his arms over his chest and looked at Holt. "What are you up to this morning? I thought you needed to go into town for something."

Holt shook his head. "I decided that could wait. I wanted to talk to you about the horse sale coming up this weekend at Tucson."

"I wasn't aware there was one. Why? Are you planning on going?"

"It's been on my mind. There's about six head in the catalog that interest me. And I'd like to replace those five mares I sold to Isabelle."

"Fine with me," Blake told him. "You know you don't have to ask me before you spend Three Rivers' money."

Holt chuckled. "Until it comes to an equine pool."

Blake groaned. "You're never going to hush about that, are you?"

"Probably not. I can always use it to irritate you."

A sly grin crossed Blake's face. "Speaking of Isabelle, I haven't had a chance to talk to you about this, but Matthew tells me that you sent Ollie and Sol over to Isabelle's ranch to work for her."

"That's right. I figured it would be easier for us to find day workers than it would be for Isabelle. She only knows a handful of people around here. And that ranch of hers is so isolated I didn't want riffraff out there with her."

Blake shrugged. "Well, I don't have any beef about them working for her. But they're still on the payroll here at Three Rivers and—"

"Uh, I'd like for you to keep it that way, Blake. I promised the men they'd keep getting their Three Rivers' paycheck—because Isabelle can only afford part-time help right now."

Blake leaned forward and stared at his brother. "I'm not sure I got this straight," he said. "Ollie and Sol are working for Isabelle, but we're paying them? And she went along with it?"

Grimacing, Holt shook his head. "Isabelle knows nothing about this setup, Blake. And I don't want her to know. She'd have a fit and send the men packing."

"I don't get this—or you, Holt! I—"

"Don't get all het up about this, Blake. Just take the amount of their pay out of my monthly salary. I'll never miss it."

Blake's mouth fell open and he studied Holt for long moments before he finally let out a heavy sigh of surrender. "Okay. Whatever you do with your money is none of my business. But—"

"But what? Go ahead and say it, brother," Holt muttered in a sardonic voice. "You think I've lost my mind or worse."

"What could be worse than losing your mind?" Blake shot the question at him.

Falling in love, Holt thought. But he wasn't doing that. No. Not by a long shot. He simply wanted Isabelle to be protected. He wanted someone there to help her. He wanted her to achieve her dreams and not be hurt along the way. That's all there was to it.

"Well, getting tangled up with a woman."

Blake's brows arched upward. "Are you getting tangled up with Isabelle?" he asked, then with a shake of his head, he rose to his feet and crossed the room to where a utility table was loaded with a coffee machine and all kinds of snacks.

As he poured himself a cup of coffee, he went on, "Don't bother to answer that, Holt. You've already told me that you're more than tangled."

"I have? How so? Just because I sent Ollie and Sol over to help her?" Holt snorted. "Can't a man help a woman out without sex or love or anything like that being involved?"

"With you, Holt, we can safely rule out the love. But the sex is another matter and I—"

Annoyed that Blake was assuming he'd already been sleeping in Isabelle's bed, he barked back at him, "You what? I really don't have time for a lecture on women this morning, Blake. Besides, who are you to give me advice about women? You were lucky enough to literally run into your wife on the sidewalk. You didn't have to date dozens and dozens of women to find Katherine. You didn't have to wonder if she was marrying you for the Hollister money, or just because she liked having sex with you!"

Blake coughed loudly. "You're taking my concern all wrong, brother. I don't want you to get hurt, that's all."

"Since when has a woman ever hurt me?" Holt countered with the question. "Not once. And it's not going to happen this time. I'm just trying to help Isabelle. She's a fellow horse trainer and I admire her ambition and courage. I like her. That's all."

Blake rolled his eyes toward the ceiling, then looked at Holt and grunted with amusement. "You like her enough to pay her ranch hands' wages. I'd hate to see what you'd spend on her if you really loved her."

If he really loved her. Holt didn't know about love. Other than the kind he felt for his mother and siblings. He wasn't sure he'd recognize the emotion if it whammed him in the face.

"Don't worry, Blake, I'm not going to

make the foolish mistake of falling in love with Isabelle. Be pretty hard to do anyway, for a man without a heart."

"Who says you don't have a heart?"

Holt wiped a hand over his face in an effort to swipe away the image of Isabelle's face when he'd left her house two nights ago. She'd looked angry, hurt, and shocked all at once. He figured right about now she'd be the first one to say he was a heartless man.

To answer Blake's question, he made a point of looking at his watch. "I'm not sure I have enough time to go down the list."

Blake shook his head and walked over to the window to peer out at the rain.

"So what was Mom doing in here?" Holt asked. "Didn't you talk to her at breakfast?"

"No. I missed breakfast. Kat needed help with the twins while she was getting ready for work." He pulled the cord to the blinds until the large window was uncovered. "Mom stopped by to discuss the cost of replacing a bull down at Red Bluff. He's getting too old to service the cows, but you know Mom. She doesn't want to sell him. He's going to be put out to pasture for the rest of his life."

"Oh. I thought she might've mentioned her trip to Phoenix the other day. Or Dad's case."

Blake glanced over his shoulder at Holt. "She didn't mention the trip. And you know good and well that she stopped talking about dad's case a long time ago. And I have no intention of bringing up the subject."

"I'm worried about her."

Blake shrugged, then walked over to his desk and eased a hip onto one corner. "I'm trying not to be. Whatever is going on in Mom's head will straighten itself out eventually. Our mother is a wise woman, Holt. We have to trust the choices she makes."

Holt wasn't too good at trusting. Especially when it involved women.

"What about Joe?" Holt asked. "Is he going out searching this week?"

At least one day a week, their brother Joseph came over to the ranch to ride the area where they believed their father had initially met his demise. Usually Blake rode with him, but sometimes Holt went instead. So far they'd found several pieces of evidence. Joel's spur rowel, a silver belt tip, and a small tattered piece of the shirt he'd been wearing that fateful day.

"He'll be over this afternoon. This rain won't last more than ten minutes anyway."

"Do you want me to ride with him this time?" Holt offered. "I can spare a few hours. And I only have about five two-year-olds to ride today."

Blake shook his head. "Thanks, Holt. But I'll go. Flo will take care of things here. And it gives me a chance to get on the back of a horse. I kinda get tired of being in an executive chair for most of the day."

Holt rose from the chair and started to the door. "I'd hate to think I had to trade that chair for a saddle."

Blake said, "Holt, about the sale, buy as many horses as you want. I trust your judgment completely."

Blake trusted his judgment with horses, just not with women, Holt thought wryly. Well, that hardly mattered. One of these days, his family was finally going to accept that he wasn't cut out to be a family man.

"Thanks, Blake. I'll keep the buying within reason. Good luck this afternoon on the search. Maybe this time you'll unearth something definitive."

"I pray you're right, little brother."

That afternoon on Blue Stallion Ranch, Isabelle picked up a lame gelding's front foot and used the handle of the hoof pick to gently peck on the sole. When the animal flinched on a certain spot, she examined it closer but failed to see anything out of the ordinary.

"This seems to be the area that's bothering her," she said as Ollie and Sol peered closely over her shoulder. "What does it look like to you guys?"

Ollie was the first to answer. "Don't see a thing, Isabelle."

"Could be a stone bruise," Sol added his thoughts on the matter.

"Can I be of help?"

The sound of Holt's voice momentarily stunned her. She'd not seen or heard from him since the other night when he'd hightailed it off the ranch like a demon was after him.

Slowly, she lowered the horse's foot back to the stall floor, while the men turned to greet their visitor.

"Hello, Holt," Ollie said. "You couldn't have shown up at a better time."

"Yeah, Isabelle's gelding is lame," Sol

added. "Maybe you can figure out the problem."

Isabelle cleared her throat. "Holt isn't the vet at Three Rivers, his brother Chandler is. I'll load the horse in the trailer and take him to the Hollister Animal Hospital," she told the two men.

Holt entered the stall and shouldered his way between Ollie and Sol to stand next to Isabelle. She forced herself to look up at him and as soon as her gaze clashed with, her heart lurched into a rapid thud. Every moment of the past two days had been haunted by the memory of his kiss and how incredible it had felt to be in his arms. Now, she could only wonder how long he'd be here before the urge to run hit him again.

"Let me take a look first," Holt suggested. "I might be able to figure out the problem."

A part of her wanted to tell him to get lost, while the other part was jumping for joy at the sight of him. Dear Lord, the man had turned her into a bundle of con-tradictions.

"If you don't mind," she said. "Any help is appreciated."

She stepped to one side to give him room to work. Behind her, Ollie and Sol moved backward until they were both resting their shoulders against the wall of the stall.

"Did this come on the horse all of a sud-den or did it start out barely noticeable and progress into a full-blown limp?" he asked.

"I'm not sure," she told him. "The last day I rode him, which was three days ago, he was fine. Then I turned him out to pasture with a few of the mares. When I got him up today to ride him, he could barely walk."

"Hmm. So you've not ridden him in the past few days?"

"No. And he's never had laminitis or arthritis or anything like that."

Holt picked up the gelding's foot and

began to put pressure on the outside wall of the hoof. When he hit a certain spot, the horse tried to jerk away from Holt's tight grip.

"It's okay, boy. You're going to be all right." He lowered the animal's foot back to the floor and gently stroked his neck before he turned to Isabelle. "Like you said, I'm not a vet, but Chandler will tell you that I can doctor horses. This one is developing an abscess. Either a small foreign particle has entered his foot through the sole or it's been bruised or injured by striking it against something hard."

"So what happens now? Do I need to take him into your brother's clinic for treatment?"

"Maybe not. You might be able to treat him yourself. Do you have any soaking salts?"

"Yes."

"What about oral painkiller for horses?"

She nodded. "I always keep it on supply."

"Great," he said. "We'll start out by giving him a dose of painkiller and then his foot needs to be soaked for at least twenty minutes twice a day. Eventually, a spot near the hairline will burst open. But don't worry. That's a good thing. It relieves the pressure of the abscess and whatever is inside will run out."

Wanting to believe it was that simple of a problem, but still doubting, she asked, "You really think that's what it is?"

"I'd bet every dollar I own," he told her, then gave her a reassuring wink. "I have a supply of antibiotics in the truck you can give him to help with the infection. In a few days, he'll be fine."

"Don't worry, Isabelle." Ollie spoke up. "Holt knows what he's doing. He's an expert on horses."

"You stay here with Holt," Sol added. "We'll go fetch everything from the tack room."

The two men left to gather what was

needed to treat the horse and Isabelle took a cautious step back from Holt.

"I think I'll go help Ollie and Sol," she said. "They might not be able to find the phenylbutazone."

She started to leave the stall, but he quickly reached out and caught her by the forearm. "Wait, Isabelle. I want to talk to you before the men return."

Her nostrils flared as she looked down at the strong fingers encircling her arm. "Look, I'm grateful for your help with my horse, Holt. But I'm not sure I want to talk with you about anything personal. That's over! Not that it ever started," she said in a brittle voice.

His fingers eased on her arm and Isabelle forced herself to lift her gaze up to his. The dark, bewildered look in his green eyes confused her.

He said, "I thought by now that you'd be wanting to thank me for leaving when I did."

"What is that supposed to mean?" she asked flatly.

He made a sound of frustration as he stepped closer. Isabelle told herself she really should pull away from him and run to the tack room and the safety of Ollie's and Sol's company. But something about Holt mesmerized her and chipped away the anger and hurt she'd been carrying around with her the past two days.

"It means that whatever was happening between us was getting out of hand— really fast. I wanted you to have time to take a breath and think about me and you. I wanted to give myself time to think about what was happening."

His voice was like the low, soft purr of a cat and the sound slowly and surely lured her to him. Closing her eyes, she rested her palms against his chest. "You're right. It was a quick explosion. But I—wished you had stayed long enough to explain. Running off like that was—not good."

His hands gently wrapped around her

upper arms. "I'm sorry, Isabelle. I realize it probably made me look like a jackass. But if I'd stayed a second longer, I couldn't have stopped kissing you or—anything else. Don't you understand? For once in my life, I was trying to be a gentleman."

How could she stay annoyed with him when the simple touch of his hands was melting every cell inside of her? She couldn't. No more than she could resist the urge to be near him.

"I didn't know that, Holt. And why has it taken you this long to explain?"

His expression rueful, he shook his head. "Saying I'm sorry doesn't come easy for me, Isabelle. And when I do apologize, it never comes out sounding right. If you want the truth, I had to work up my courage to come over here."

Suddenly tears were stinging the backs of her eyes and she turned her back to him and swallowed hard. Something about his words and the way he'd said them had struck her in a deep, vulnerable spot.

She sniffed and said, "If you want the truth, I'm glad you're here. I just—"

"You felt like you needed to take me to task a bit," he finished for her. "I understand. I don't blame you."

Smiling now, she turned to face him. "It doesn't matter. I forgive you. And hopefully you've forgiven me."

Surprise arched his brows. "For what?"

Her cheeks felt as though they were flaming. "For acting like that kiss of ours was—something more than just a pleasant, physical connection."

His green gaze made a slow survey of her face. "Is that what you think it was? Just a physical reaction?"

Actually, Isabelle still wasn't sure what had happened between them or how they'd gone from a simple kiss to an explosion of passion. To her, it had been like nothing she'd ever experienced with any man. But she'd never admit such a thing to him.

Making love to a woman was second nature to Holt. He knew exactly how to make her feel special. Even loved. Isabelle wasn't going to be so stupid as to think Holt could ever have a serious thought about her. With him, everything was physical and that's all she was going to allow herself to feel about him.

"I'm positive it was," she answered.

He let out a long breath and Isabelle figured it was a sign of great relief.

"I see," he said. "Well, that's good. Because neither of us want strings between us."

Foolish pain squeezed the middle of her chest, but she smiled in spite of it. "No. No strings. I believe we can enjoy each other's company without any of those, don't you?"

Surprise, or something like it, flickered in his eyes and then he smiled back at her. "Absolutely."

There, she thought. She'd fixed everything. He believed that kiss had meant nothing more to her than a few moments of physical pleasure. Now, all she had to do was convince herself.

A half hour later, with the gelding treated and turned out to a small lot near the barn, Holt and Isabelle stood outside the fence observing the horse as he walked gingerly toward a hay manger.

The rain had cleared and bright sunshine was warming the muddy ground around the ranch yard. It was turning into a beautiful day, Holt thought. Especially now that Isabelle was smiling at him again.

She asked, "Would you like to walk to the house and have a cup of coffee? I'd offer you what was left of the blueberry pie, but I gave it to Ollie and Sol. I do have brownies, though. That's the least I can do for your vet services."

He put a finger to his lips and made a shushing noise. "Don't say that out loud.

Chandler will have my hide for practicing without a license."

Isabelle laughed. "I'm sure," she said drolly. "He's probably grateful for the help."

"He does have too much to do," Holt agreed. "And I do, too. As much as I'd like the coffee, I'd better head on back to town. I actually need to stop by the clinic and pick up a few things we need at the ranch."

She rested her back against the board fence and jammed her hands in the pockets of her brown work jacket. In dress clothes, she looked like a glamour girl, yet she'd chosen a very unglamorous job for herself. She was such a paradox and he had to admit that everything about the woman fascinated him.

"You know, I do have a cell phone," she said. "You could've called to apologize."

There was an impish curve to her lips that made Holt want to snatch her into his arms and kiss her. But now was hardly the time when Ollie or Sol could walk up on them at any moment.

"I thought you said you were glad I came."

"I am," she replied. "I'm just wondering why you took the time to drive all the way out here."

He casually rested one shoulder next to hers. "It's always better to be face-to-face when you tell someone you're sorry for being a jerk. But I also have something else on my mind to talk to you about."

Her blue eyes widened a fraction, but she didn't bother to look at him. Instead she kept her gaze on the open land stretching away from the barn area. He wondered if that far-off look had anything to do with him or if she was simply thinking about this ranch and all that she wanted it to be.

Blue Stallion Ranch. She hadn't found her blue stallion yet, but she was already building her dream around him, he thought. Holt hadn't forgotten how she'd practically begged him to sell his roan colt, Blue Midnight, to her. Nor had he forgotten the instant bond she'd made with the stallion. If it had been any colt but that one, he would have been more than happy to sell to her. But his future was wrapped around that horse. He couldn't give him up just to make Isabelle happy.

"What is it you wanted to talk to me about?" she asked, breaking into his thoughts. "You want me to cook for you again?"

He laughed. "No. I wanted to invite you to take a trip with me. There's a horse sale going on at Tucson this coming Saturday. The horses are all registered and cataloged. I thought you might enjoy it. You might even want to purchase something."

That turned her head in his direction and she pondered his face for long moments before she finally replied, "I would enjoy it. Does it take very long to drive down there?"

"From Wickenburg, it takes about three hours or a little over. But it's a nice drive and if you've never seen the Tucson area, it's very pretty."

"I've not been to that part of the state before. I'd love to see it. And I suppose I could take my checkbook. Just in case I saw a horse I like. Who knows, I might even find that blue stallion I want," she added with a clever smile.

"Did you ever see a horse you didn't like?" he teased.

She laughed. "I think you're beginning to know me, Holt."

And he was beginning to like her more and more, he thought. Asking her to join him on the trip to Tucson was like inviting trouble to walk right up and sock him in the jaw. But he'd never been one to take the safe route. Not even where a woman was concerned.

"So can I plan on you going?"

"Sure. How could I possibly refuse a day of horses and—you?"

Holt wasn't sure whether she was being serious or sardonic. Either way, it didn't matter. The playful twinkle in her blue eyes was enough for him.

"Great. The sale starts at ten so I thought we might meet at Chandler's clinic around six and leave from there. That way we'll have about an hour to look over the horses before the auction begins."

She pushed away from the fence. "I'll be there."

"See you then." Smiling, he bent and placed a swift kiss on her cheek.

"Saturday. Six o'clock. Don't leave without me," she said.

Feeling like he'd just stepped onto a cloud, Holt laughed and started the short walk to his truck. "Not a chance," he called back to her.

Chapter Eight

That night, after a long shower and a plate of leftovers, Isabelle carried her phone and a cup of coffee to the couch in the living room and punched her mother's number.

Gabby didn't answer and Isabelle hung up, thinking she'd probably already gone to bed for the night. But after a couple of minutes, the phone rang with her mother's returning call.

"Did I wake you?" Isabelle asked. "I didn't realize it was getting so late."

"You didn't wake me. I just got back

in the apartment. I was over at the Green Garden going over some things with Carl about the showing."

"How's that working out? Is everything still on go?"

"Yes! I'm really getting revved up about this, Issy. I'm thinking this might give me a giant step forward."

Isabelle felt a pang of guilt, but only a small one. "Well, the showing is what I'm calling about. I was planning on flying down this weekend, but I've had something else come up."

Her mother paused, then groaned. "All at once, you've managed to make me happy and sad. I'm thrilled that you were coming and sad that you aren't. I hope that whatever has come up is important."

Isabelle had to be honest. "I don't know about being important, but it's something I want to do. I'm going to a horse sale down at Tucson—with a friend."

"A friend? Male or female?"

Isabelle drew her legs up beneath her while wondering what her mother would think about Holt if she actually met him. That her daughter was playing with fire? She wouldn't be wrong, Isabelle thought.

"A man. The rancher I went to dinner with. The one who sold the mares to me. Remember?"

"Yes. I remember. I think you said his name was Holt something or other."

"Hollister. They own half this county and more."

Gabby was slow to reply and when she did Isabelle noticed a thread of concern in her voice. "Issy, I've been praying you'd find someone else. But I honestly can't say I'm getting good vibes about you seeing this man. Trevor had too much money and it sounds like this one does, too. Don't you think you'd be happier if you found a poor ole Joe? One that would focus on you instead of padding his bank account?"

"I don't think Holt's that way about

making money. Yes, when it comes to his horses, he's a workaholic. But I don't think wealth is all that important to him. And anyway, I'm not getting serious about him, Mom. He's just a man that I enjoy being with."

"That's the worst kind. You get to enjoying it so much you never want to be without him."

Isabelle wasn't going to let herself get that attached to Holt Hollister. When she did finally open her heart and allow a man to step inside, it was going to be one who was yearning for the same things that she was longing for. A home and children together. Their old age spent together.

"That isn't going to happen, Mom. He's not the serious type. And after what I went through with Trevor, that's just the kind I need right now."

There was another long pause from her mother and then she said, "Okay, you're a grown woman and I'm not going to try to run your love life. I am curious about one thing, though. You said you were planning on flying down—what about the horses? Have you finally hired some ranch hands?"

Isabelle told her all about Ollie and Sol and what a great help they'd been to her, then ended with describing the bunkroom she'd helped them construct in the barn.

"Oh, so the men are staying on the ranch full time. That's great, honey. I can stop worrying about you living out there alone now."

I won't be worrying about you so much.

Holt's comment had taken Isabelle by complete surprise. It had almost made him sound like he cared about her.

Don't start going there, Isabelle. Holt only cares about himself and his family. And you're not a part of the Hollister family. You never will be.

"Isabelle? Are you still there?"

Her mother's question pushed away the warring voices in Isabelle's head. "Yes,

Mom. I'm here. I was just thinking—you never mentioned that you worried about me."

"You've had enough to deal with these past few months without listening to a whiny mother. But sometimes I—wish you would've decided to stay here with me in San Diego. It would've been a cinch for you to have gotten your old job back with the energy company. You made a humongous salary there. And the stables where you boarded your horses weren't all that expensive. You had a nice life here until—"

For some reason, Isabelle looked over at the cushion where Holt had sat next to her. Just having him here with her in front of the warm fire, listening to his voice, and watching the subtle expressions play across his face had been so nice and special. Then when he'd reached for her, she'd been shocked and thrilled. In a matter of moments, she'd wanted to take him by the hand and lead him straight to her bed.

Shaking her head, she tried to focus on her mother's remarks. "Until I met Trevor. Isn't that what you were going to say?"

"Yes, but—forget I said any of that. It's just that I miss you."

"I made a foolish choice when I married Trevor. But as for me ever moving back to San Diego—that isn't going to happen. I love my ranch, my land. Someday it's going to be the home I always wanted."

"Complete with horses and children," Gabby said, her voice tender. "That's really all I want for you, honey, to be happy and loved by a man. God knows your father never really loved me. Not as much as he did his piano. But that's okay. He gave me you. And that's a priceless gift."

A lump of emotion was suddenly burning Isabelle's throat. "Oh, Mom, you're making me cry. I'm hanging up—I'll call you later."

"Good night, Issy. And have a nice time with your rancher."

Isabelle ended the call, then left the

couch and walked over to the picture window. From this angle, she could see a portion of the main barn and a light burning in the small window of Ollie and Sol's bunkroom.

Knowing the men were there was a comfort to her. Yet they couldn't fill up the emptiness in the house or in her heart.

To be happy and loved by a man, that's what her mother wished for her. And that was all Isabelle had ever really wanted. Not money or travels or a glamorous social life. Just a loving, caring man at her side. But would she ever find that man?

Not with Holt, she thought sadly.

But that didn't mean she couldn't enjoy his company. And that was exactly what she intended to do.

At half past eleven that night, Holt was still in the foaling barn, carefully watching the newly born filly wobble to her feet and begin to nose her mother's flank. Eventually, she found one of the warm teats and he smiled with satisfaction as the baby latched on and began to nurse hungrily.

He was still watching the pair when Chandler's voice suddenly broke the quietness of the barn. "I ran in to T.J. heading to the bunkhouse. He told me you were in here."

Holt glanced over his shoulder to see his brother entering the large stall. "What the hell are you doing down here at this hour? You should be in bed with Roslyn," he scolded.

Shaking his head, Chandler came to stand next to him. "I couldn't sleep. I didn't want my tossing to disturb Roslyn and I was a little concerned that you might need me to help with the mare. You've been out here at the barn too long."

"The mare seemed to make it okay. But from my records, I think she's delivered a bit early. Maybe that's a good thing, though. Look how big the foal is. Mama might have had real trouble if she'd carried it any longer."

Chandler carefully moved closer to the bay mare and matching filly. "The baby looks good and strong, Holt. No matter about the due dates. Mother Nature always knows best. Since I'm here anyway, do you want me to check them over? Just to make sure?"

"I'd feel better if you would," Holt told him.

Chandler approached the new mother and daughter and went to work examining both. Once he was satisfied with his findings, he folded the stethoscope he'd carried with him and jammed it back into the pocket on his jacket.

"Both of them are fit as fiddles," he pronounced.

Holt slapped a hand on Chandler's broad shoulder. "Thanks, brother. Now get back to the house and go to bed."

"I'm not ready for bed."

"Hell, it's almost midnight. And you have a busy day tomorrow." Holt took a second look at his brother's taut features and decided there had to be more to his showing up here at the foaling barn at such a late hour. "Okay, what's wrong?"

Chandler patted the mare's neck, then moved to the opposite side of the stall. "Nothing is wrong. Well, not exactly," he mumbled. "Hell, I'm not sure what I'm feeling right now."

"There's a crease in the middle of your forehead as a big as the Grand Canyon." Holt gestured to the stall door. "Let's go to my office. I think there's some coffee still on the hot plate. You can tell me what's on your mind."

Chandler nodded. "I'll pass on your syrupy coffee, but there is something we need to talk about."

The two brothers left the foaling barn and entered the end of the main horse barn where Holt's office was located. After both men were seated and Holt was nursing a cup of the strong coffee, Chandler closed his eyes and passed a hand over his forehead.

"Man, you must really be down about something," Holt commented as he carefully studied his brother's miserable expression. "Are you and Roslyn having problems? Has her father been making waves?"

"No. It's nothing about Roslyn. And miracle of miracles, Martin seems to be getting softer as time goes by. He's already talking about coming out for another visit this spring."

Holt let out a humorous snort. "Maybe you'd better prescribe yourself some horse calmer before he arrives."

Chandler grunted. "My father-in-law won't give me any problems. Anyway, it's the Hollister family that's worrying me now. Joseph just left the house a few minutes ago."

Totally puzzled, Holt leaned forward. "Joe went home earlier this afternoon—after he and Blake got back from their ride. I heard Joe say they didn't find anything. He came back over here tonight? For what?"

Chandler pulled off his hat and raked both hands through his hair. Since he rarely showed signs of stress, his unusual behavior was making Holt uneasy.

"When Joe got back to the Bar X, he found Tessa in one of her cleaning moods and asked him to carry some boxes down from the attic. She's slowly been trying to sift through all the things that Ray had stored up there before he died."

"So what happened?"

Chandler clapped his hat back on his head. "The two of them were digging through some old papers and correspondence and happened to run into a notebook filled with logs about Dad's case."

Holt's jaw dropped. "Seriously? This sounds too far out to be real, Chandler."

"I can assure you it is real. Joe brought the notebook over and showed it to me and Blake."

"Hell, I leave the house for three hours

and all of this happens," Holt muttered. "So what did it say? We've been hoping and praying for a break in uncovering the truth. Is there anything in there that's going to help?"

Chandler shook his head again. "We don't know. Maybe. One thing is for sure, if the evidence gets out, it's going to cause a hell of a storm."

Stunned, Holt stared at him. As sheriff of Yavapai County, Ray Maddox had ruled, for lack of evidence, Joel's death an accident. But their old friend had never actually quit investigating the incident.

"Evidence? I thought we had everything Ray had gathered."

"I shouldn't have called it evidence. It's not that exactly," Chandler told him. "It's more like a break that might lead to solving the case. Ray kept some things to himself."

"Why would he do such a thing? Ray and Dad were like brothers. He wanted to expose the truth about Dad's death just as much as we do."

Chandler heaved out a long breath. "We suppose he hid the info because he couldn't connect it with anything. And given the nature of it, he probably figured it would cause more harm than good. But damn it, he should have told us. Mom didn't have to know then. And she sure as hell isn't going to know now. Not unless we put two and two together and come up with a feasible explanation."

"I'm in the dark here, Chandler. Maybe you'd better tell me exactly what you found in these notes of Ray's."

Chandler glanced away from Holt and swallowed as though he was trying to get down a handful of roofing nails. "From Ray's notes, he believed that Dad was meeting a woman on a regular basis at the stockyards in Phoenix."

Holt couldn't have felt more dazed if the ceiling of the barn had crashed in on his head. "What?"

"That's right. The same finding was entered several times in the notebook. More than once, Joel had been observed in the company of a blond woman. Petite in build and about the same age as him. Whoever gave Ray this information must not have known the status of their relationship, because Ray didn't mention any of that. Ray scribbled down a list of dates with the word *Phoenix* written out to the side. One of the dates was a day after Dad's death."

Holt's mind was racing with a thousand questions and just as many possible answers. "The stockyards. A day after Dad's death," he mused out loud. "Chandler, a year or so ago, Mom found that old agenda book of Dad's. There's a note in it, saying he was to meet a man at the stockyards on that day. Joe researched the man's name and learned the name was phony. Maybe it wasn't a man Dad was planning on meeting that day, but rather the blond woman?"

"It's possible. But why would Dad have been so deceitful about it? Why would he put down a man's name if it had been a woman he was meeting? Mother never was the jealous kind. If he'd been meeting a woman for a business lunch or something of that sort, she wouldn't have cared."

Holt felt sick inside, then immediately felt guilty for even doubting his father's fidelity for one minute. "I don't know what you and Joe and Blake think. But as far as I'm concerned, I don't believe there was any sort of romantic involvement between Dad and this woman. Yes, he probably was seeing her and what that reason might have been is a big question mark. But he wasn't cheating on Mom. Dad wasn't made like that. He was an honorable man. A family man. And he loved Mom more than anything on this earth. Even more than Three Rivers and that's saying a lot."

Chandler blew out another heavy breath. "Yeah, that's what I think, too. I'm not sure what Blake thinks. You know how he is, he keeps most of his thoughts to himself. The important ones, at least. Joe is different, he sees things as a lawman. He weighs the evidence in an analytical way. And during his tenure as a deputy, Joe has witnessed some shocking things. I don't think he'd be that surprised to discover our father had been having an affair. After all, think how stunned everyone one was when we learned that Ray was really Tessa's father."

Holt swigged down a mouthful of the gritty coffee. "That's true. But Ray's wife was wheelchair bound. They had no children. That was no excuse for him having an affair, but I can kind of see why it happened. But Dad had a beautiful, vibrant wife with six children. He had no reason to have an affair."

Chandler eyed him for several pointed moments. "I'm surprised to hear you say that. You love women. I thought you didn't have to have a reason to have an affair. Other than lust."

"Damn it, Chandler, that's a low, low blow."

"Oh, come off it, Holt. Righteousness doesn't fit you."

"Thanks. Being noble was never my goal in life," he said sarcastically. "Just give me faster horses and more women and I'll die a happy man."

He tossed the remainder of his coffee into a trash basket and replaced the glass cup next to the coffee maker.

Behind him, Chandler groaned. "Okay, that was a low blow. I'm sorry."

"Forget it. I can admit that I'll never be like my brothers. I'm not cut out for it, Chandler. But that doesn't mean I'm a tomcat with no feelings or discretion." He wiped a hand over his face as Isabelle's image tried to push itself to the front of his brain. "Oh, God, brother, what if we're wrong about Dad? What if he was cheating on our mother and an enraged husband or boyfriend killed him? Mom would be—well, I don't want to think of what that might do to her."

Chandler looked resolute. "Listen, none of us are going to breathe a word of this to Mom. She's already been having too many melancholy moods. This might send her into a tailspin."

"What does Joe intend to do with this bit of information?" Holt asked. "You suggested it might be a break in the case. But how? It's been years since Dad died. It would be miraculous if anyone remembers anything."

"Joe is going to keep asking questions. He believes he'll eventually find a cattle buyer or worker at the stockyards who might remember something about Dad and the woman."

Holt's stomach gave another sickening lurch. "I understand now why Mom doesn't want to search for the cause or reason of Dad's death. The truth might make everything worse."

His expression grim, Chandler rose to his feet. "If we find that Dad was living a secret life, we're going to bury the facts. No one will know except us four brothers."

Holt couldn't believe Chandler was even considering the possibility that Ray's speculations could be true, much less that they should hide the truth from their sisters. "And not tell Viv and Camille? Chandler, your thinking is all mixed up!"

"If I'm confused, then so are Blake and Joe, because they think the same thing. Viv and Camille adored Dad. He was their hero. Nothing good would come from crushing their ideals and memories."

Their father had been Holt's hero, too. He'd gotten his love of horses from Joel and his ability to laugh at the challenges that training them presented. Had he also inherited a straying eye for the ladies from his father?

No! Until Holt's dying day, he'd always believe Joel Hollister was a true husband and father.

* * *

Isabelle gazed out the passenger window of Holt's truck at the desert hills covered with tall saguaros and areas of thick chaparral and slab rock. In the past few minutes, the sun had dipped behind a ridge of mountains to the west and shadows were painting the rugged landscape. It was a lovely sight, she thought. A fitting close to the beautiful day she'd spent in Holt's company.

"Are you sure you didn't mind leaving the auction early?"

Holt's question broke into her pleasant thoughts and she glanced over to where he sat behind the steering wheel, driving them toward Wickenburg. Throughout the day, he'd never left her side and during all that time, their hands had brushed, their shoulders rubbed. The touches had been incidental, but to Isabelle they'd felt like the sizzling contact of a branding iron.

Now, with each passing minute, she felt a connection growing between them.

Whether the link was emotional, sexual, or something in between, she couldn't determine. And she wasn't going to ruin the remainder of their trip trying to figure it out.

"I didn't mind at all. Each of us already purchased two mares," she said pointedly, then chuckled. "And leaving when we did probably saved me a few thousand dollars. I would've probably gotten into a bidding war for that buckskin colt that caught my eye."

"Just about every horse at the auction caught your eye," he said.

"I'm guilty. I confess. Mom always said I never saw a horse I didn't love."

"I'm curious about your mother," he replied. "Where did she get her knowledge about horses?"

"From her parents—my grandparents. They owned a small ranch near Bishop and Granddad was an excellent horseman."

"Are your grandparents still living?"

"No. Granddad died from complications of diabetes. When he passed, Grandmother was in still in fairly good shape, but losing him took a toll on her. They'd been married for more than fifty-five years and she wasn't the same with Granddad gone. She died about a year after he did." She glanced at him. "What about your grandparents, Holt? I don't think I've heard you mention them."

He shook his head. "Both sets are gone now. My Hollister grandparents lived and worked on the ranch all their lives. They both died of different ailments when I was in elementary school. My mom's parents lived in another state and we didn't see them very often. Her father passed away from a stroke and her mother died from a car accident. It was just a little fender bender, but she wasn't wearing her seat belt and her head hit the windshield." He reached over and slipped a forefinger beneath her belt and gave it a tug. "That's why I want you to promise me that you'll always buckle up."

Did he really care about her safety that much? No. She couldn't let herself go down that path. No serious strings. No thinking about love or the future, she scolded herself.

She forced a little laugh past her throat. "I promise. But we don't have safety belts on our saddles."

"No, we just have to hang on tighter." The grin on his face disappeared as he slanted her another glance. "I'm sorry you didn't find a blue stallion for your ranch, Isabelle. I was hoping you would."

He honestly seemed to care about her dreams and wishes. Something that Trevor never bothered to do. Oh, he'd wanted her to be happy, but he was never interested in the things that were most important to her. He'd thought handing her a check to a limitless bank account was enough to make up for his indifference. Maybe that should have been enough for her, but it hadn't been. She'd felt like an afterthought, something to be petted and admired and placed back on a shelf.

"That's okay," she told him. "Blue roans are not that plentiful. That's one of the reasons why they're so sought after and expensive. The two that we watched go through the ring weren't that great. I'll find my stallion someday."

"There's always a chance Blue Midnight will throw some nice colts. I won't forget I promised you a shot to buy one."

She smiled at him. "That's a long time off, but I'll hold you to your promise."

He didn't reply and for the next few miles Isabelle could see he was deep in thought about something. Was it her, the horses, or something too personal to share with her? Was he thinking about some other woman he'd rather be with? No. If he wanted to be with some other woman, he wouldn't have invited Isabelle to join him today. At least she could take comfort in that.

Minutes later, the lights of Wickenburg appeared on the dark horizon and Isabelle realized she was dreading telling Holt good-night. She didn't want this special day to end, or her time with him to be over.

They had passed through the small town and were nearing Hollister Animal Hospital when Isabelle questioned an earlier plan they'd made to deal with getting the two horses she'd purchased home to Blue Stallion Ranch.

"Now that I think about it, Holt, leaving my horses overnight at the clinic barn isn't such a good idea. They haven't been quarantined. They could pass shipping fever to Chandler's patients and I'd feel very guilty if that happened. Not to mention how angry it would make him. I can drive home, pick up my trailer, and be back in an hour or so to collect them."

His attention remained focused on the highway. "Don't fret about it, Isabelle. We're not leaving your horses or mine at the clinic. I'm going to take all four of them out to your ranch."

She sat straight up and stared at him. "Oh. But I thought—"

He arched a questioning brow in her direction. "The four of them have been trailered together for the past three and half hours. Penning them together tonight won't hurt. I'll leave mine at your place and haul them home to Three Rivers in a few days. That is, if you don't mind."

"Um—no. I don't mind."

That meant Holt would be following her home to Blue Stallion Ranch. After they tended the horses, would he want to stay? Or was he worried that if he let her get too close, she might try to throw a lariat on him?

The notion of any woman trying to tie Holt down was ridiculous. He was a maverick. But even mavericks needed love sometimes, she mentally argued. And tonight he just might decide he needed her.

Chapter Nine

During the twenty-minute drive to Isabelle's ranch, Holt tried not to think past getting the mares comfortably settled, but he knew the smart thing to do would be to kiss her and tell her goodbye. But the kiss would have to be on the cheek, not her lips. Otherwise, he'd be totally and completely lost to her.

And what would be wrong with that, Holt? This day with Isabelle has been more than special for you. It's been a game changer. She's no longer just a sexy female you want to bed. You want much more from her. Like her company and friendship and—

Muttering a curse, he reached over and turned up the volume on the radio in an effort to drown out the voice in his head. Tonight wasn't the time to let his heart do his thinking for him. If Isabelle was ready to invite him into her bed, he'd be a fool to turn her down. It was that simple.

When he braked the truck to a stop near Isabelle's barn, she, along with Ollie and Sol, were waiting to help. With the four of them working together, it took only a few short minutes to have the mares settled into a sheltered pen with plenty of alfalfa and water.

As Ollie and Sol headed back to the bunkhouse, Holt turned to Isabelle. "Now that we've finished that chore, how about you and me having coffee?"

Her smile flashed in the darkness. "I can probably come up with a cup of coffee."

"Only one cup?"

Her laugh was suggestive and Holt couldn't stop his thoughts from heading straight to her bedroom. But what kind of consequences would that produce? After learning his father might have been involved with another woman, Holt had been pondering on his own past. Before, he'd never really wondered if his playing the field had ever caused anyone to suffer. Now it bothered him to think that what he'd considered fun and games might have actually hurt another person.

He was getting soft, he thought sickly. He was getting all messed up in the head, and why? Because he thought his father might have been an adulterer, or because Isabelle was transforming him into a different man? Either way, Holt felt like everything around him was rapidly changing. And he was helpless to stop any of it.

"If you mind your manners, you might get two cups," Isabelle said, breaking into his thoughts. "I might even give you a brownie to go with the coffee."

"I can't wait." He curled his arm around her waist and kept it there as they walked the remaining distance to the house.

Inside the mudroom, they both shed their jackets and hung them on a hall tree. Holt added his black hat to one of the wooden arms, then followed Isabelle into the warm kitchen.

While she went to work putting the coffee makings together, Holt stood to one side, watching her graceful movements. All day long, he'd had to fight with himself to keep his eyes off the way the soft pink sweater outlined the shape of her breasts and the way her jeans cupped her pert little bottom.

Now that the two of them were completely alone, the urge to stare was turning into a need to touch. By the time she handed him a steaming cup of coffee and a brownie wrapped in a piece of wax paper, he didn't want either one. All Holt wanted was her in his arms.

"Do you want to go out to the living room?" she asked. "There's no crackling fire waiting for us, but the furniture is more comfortable."

"I can build a fire—if you'd like," he suggested.

She paused for a second, then reached for her cup. "No. That's too much trouble. And you'll be leaving soon."

Her gaze lifted to meet his and the flicker of yearning Holt spotted in the soft blue of her eyes caused his heart to do a crazy flip.

"I will?" he asked softly.

Her rose-colored lips formed a surprised O. "Uh—I thought that's what you wanted," she said, huskily. "You said you needed time to think about you and me and—"

Holt couldn't stand anymore. He placed the brownie and the cup onto the cabinet counter and reached for her. As he circled his arms around her, he murmured, "These past few days I've done a hell of a lot of thinking, Isabelle. About that kiss that blew me away—about those strings that neither of us want. And the more I think, the more everything comes down to this."

He lowered his head and covered her lips with a kiss that was just long enough to fill his loins with heat, yet short enough to keep him from losing his breath.

"Holt, I—"

"You want me. I can hear it in your voice. Taste it in your lips."

There was no indecision in her eyes as her hands came up to curl over the tops of his shoulders.

"Yes," she murmured huskily. "I do—want you—very much."

He brought his lips back to hers and she groaned as his lips moved over hers in a rough, consuming kiss. She matched the hungry movements of his mouth and in a matter of a few short seconds, Holt was out of his mind with need to have her closer.

When he finally found enough will-power to tear his mouth from hers, he could see a dazed cloud in her eyes. He was equally stunned by the passion exploding between them, and his rattled state must have flickered in his eyes.

"You're not thinking about leaving, are you?"

Tightening the circle of his arms, he said, "I couldn't leave you now even if Ollie and Sol started yelling the barn was on fire."

Her laugh was low and sexy and the erotic sound was like fingertips walking across his skin.

"I think the coffee can wait." She took his hand and led him out of the kitchen and down a long hallway to her bedroom.

There was no light on inside, but like the rest of the house, the windows were bare of curtains and the silver glow from a crescent moon was enough to illuminate a path to a queen-size bed covered with a patchwork quilt.

As soon as they reached the side of the mattress, she released her hold on his hand and slid her arms around his waist. Holt dropped his head and found her lips once again. This time he tried to keep the kiss slow and controlled, but that plan was waylaid the moment her lips began to respond to his. Like a flash fire, their embrace turned hot and out of control.

"This is going too fast, Isabelle. But I—"

Frantically, she whispered, "I don't want you to slow down." She planted quick little kisses against his jaw and throat. "I can't bear the waiting. We'll go slower the next time."

The next time. Just the idea of a second time with this woman was enough to lift the hair off his scalp.

"I can't bear the waiting either." His voice sounded like he'd been eating gravel and his hands were shaking as they skimmed down her back and onto her hips.

Having sex with Isabelle. That's all he was doing, Holt silently shouted at himself. This wasn't anything to fear. It wasn't going to change him. All it was going to do was give him pleasure. Hot, delicious pleasure.

He recognized her hands were on the front of his shirt, jerking at the pearl snaps. When the fabric parted and her palms flattened against the bare skin of his chest, he was already hard, his body aching for release.

"I, uh, better do this, Isabelle—or—we might never make it onto the bed."

With the smile of a tempting siren, she stepped aside and began to undress. Next to her, Holt hastily jerked off his boots and jeans, then added his shirt to the pile. From the corner of his eye, he saw a circle of denim pool around her bare feet. Before she could step out of it, he planted his hands on either side of her waist and lifted her backward and onto the bed.

The jeans dangled from her toes and she laughingly kicked them off as she waited for him to join her.

"You're still dressed," Holt said.

She glanced down at the black scraps of lace covering her breasts and the V between her thighs. "You should be able to handle these little ole things."

He joined her on the bed and allowed his gaze to take in the glorious sight of her nearly naked body.

"It'll be my pleasure." Propping his head up on one elbow, he used his other hand to slip over the mound of one breast, then onto the concave of her belly. "The moonlight makes you look like a silver goddess. I'm not sure that you're real. I should kiss you just to make sure."

She rolled eagerly toward him. "I'm real, Holt, and at this moment I wouldn't want to be anywhere else, except here with you."

Holt wasn't expecting her little confession to smack him in the chest, but then nothing about this time with her was how he'd thought it might be. She was making him feel vulnerable and insecure. It was crazy. Even laughable. Yet he couldn't laugh. He was too busy worrying that he was going to disappoint her.

"Isabelle." Her name came out on a whisper as he thrust his hand into her hair and allowed the white-blond strands to slide through his fingers. "I've imagined you—us—like this so many times. But I—wasn't sure it would ever happen."

"I wasn't sure I wanted it to happen."

"And now?"

Sighing, she echoed his earlier words. "I couldn't leave you if Ollie and Sol yelled the barn was on fire."

He leaned over and kissed the lids of her eyes, then moved his lips down her nose and finally onto her mouth. Her arm slipped around his waist and she tugged herself forward, until the front of her body was pressed tightly against his. The sensation of having her warm skin and soft curves next to his bare body very nearly shattered the fragile grip he held on his self-control.

He broke the kiss and scattered a trail of kisses beneath her ear and down the side of her neck until he reached the spot where pulse thumped against the soft skin. His lips lingered there, savoring the taste, before he finally claimed her mouth in another hungry search.

After that, his brain became too fuzzy to clearly perceive what the rest of his body was doing. He remembered slipping away her lingerie and his boxers, recalled her reassuring him that she was on birth control. Then the next thing he knew, his hands were cupped around her breasts and he was entering her with one urgent thrust.

Her soft cry of pleasure jolted his rattled senses and he looked down to see her face bathed in moonlight. The delicate features were almost ethereal, making him wonder if he was going to suddenly wake and discover this was an incredible dream.

But then her hips suddenly arched toward his and the reality of the moment hit him. Slowly and surely he began to move inside her and as he did, he realized his greatest fear about making love to Isabelle had happened. After this night, he'd never be the same.

This was not what Isabelle had imagined. Making love to Holt wasn't supposed to be turning the room upside down. His kisses, his touches weren't supposed to be slinging her senses to some far-off galaxy. But that was exactly what was happening.

His hands were racing over her bare skin, lighting a fire wherever his fingers dared to touch. His lips were consuming hers, while his tongue probed the sensitive area beyond her teeth. She welcomed his dominating kiss and reveled in the fact that it was melting every bone in her body.

Over and over, he thrust into her and the feeling was all so glorious, so incredible, that the pleasure was almost too intense for her to bear. And when she began to writhe frantically beneath him, he must have recognized her agony.

He tore his mouth from hers and buried his face in her tumbled hair. "Hold on, my sweet," he whispered urgently. "Just a— moment longer. A moment more—so I can give you—everything. Everything!"

With her legs wrapped around his hips, she gripped his shoulders and tried to hang on, but it was impossible to stop the white-hot tide of pleasure from washing her away.

Through the whirling haze, she heard him cry her name and felt his final thrust. She tried to breathe, but her lungs had ceased to function. And then breathing suddenly seemed superfluous as the room turned to velvety space and the both of them were drifting through an endless universe.

When Isabelle finally regained awareness, her cheek was pinned between the mattress and Holt's shoulder. With most of his weight draped over her, the pressure on her lungs made breathing even more difficult. Even so, she didn't want him to move. She wanted to hold him close for as long as he would stay.

"Sorry, Isabelle. I'm squashing you." He rolled to one side and pulled her into the curve of his warm body.

Sighing, Isabelle pillowed her head on his shoulder and closed her eyes. Neither of them spoke, but the silence was far from awkward. She was enjoying the precious sound of his breathing, the night wind blowing against the window and the faint whinnies of the mares as they accustomed themselves to their new home.

This was everything she'd ever wanted, Isabelle thought drowsily. Her ranch and a man who filled her heart to the very brim.

"I hear the mares," Holt murmured. "They've been through some changes today. They're not sure what's going to happen to them now."

Isabelle could empathize with the horses. Her life had taken a drastic change tonight, too. And she had no idea what it might do to her future or her happiness. She wanted to think that Holt might want them to remain together. Not just for a few weeks or months, but for always. And yet, she recognized that wasn't likely to happen.

Resting her palm upon his chest, she said, "They'll soon realize that they're safe."

His fingers absently played with her hair. "I've been thinking about those two mares I bought today. Do you like them?"

She slid her hand across his warm muscles until she felt the quick thump of his heart. "I love them. Next to blue roan, my favorite color is plain brown with no markings. They're almost as hard to find as the blues and today you happened to latch onto two of them. You're a lucky man, Holt."

"Yeah, like latching onto you." He pressed a kiss to the top of her head. "Now, about the mares—what would you say about keeping them here at Blue Stallion for a while? Since they're already bred, there's no need for me to put my stud on them. Maybe we could go partners on them?"

She snatched the sheet against her naked breasts and sat straight up. "Partners? Really?"

A lopsided grin spread over his face. "Yes. Really."

The grin coupled with the dark hair tousled across his forehead, along with the five o'clock shadow on his jaw, was enough to shred her focus. The subject of the mares completely left her mind as she leaned down and kissed him softly on the lips.

"Mmm. That's so nice," she said.

His hand came to rest against the back

of her head and he held her there, kissing her again, until desire began to flicker and glow deep within her.

"My suggestion about the mares? Or the kiss?" he wanted to know.

She smiled against his lips. "The kiss. And the mares. I'd love to keep them here with me."

And keep you here, too, she wanted to add. But bit back the words before they could slip out. For tonight it was enough to be in his arms.

He said, "That's what I wanted to hear."

She cupped her hands around his face. "I thought you wanted to hear it was time to finally eat those brownies we left on the counter."

A chuckle fanned her lips, and he pressed her shoulders backward until she was lying on the mattress and he was hovering over her.

"What brownies?"

Her soft laugh was instantly blotted out with a kiss.

* * *

"Wake up, sleepyhead. You're burning daylight."

The sound of Isabelle's voice caused Holt's eyes to pop open and he blinked several times before he managed to focus on her image standing at the side of the bed.

She was already dressed in jeans and boots and a blue shirt that matched her eyes. One hand was holding a cup of steaming coffee.

"Is that coffee for me?"

The smile on her face was as bright as the morning sunlight streaming through the windows.

"It is. How do you want your eggs? Fried, scrambled, or in an omelet?"

He didn't have time for eggs! He shouldn't even be here! What had he been thinking last night?

He hadn't been thinking, that's what. Making love to Isabelle and lying next to her warm body had lulled him into a quiet sense of contentment. Instead of getting up and going home, he'd fallen asleep.

He took the cup from her and swallowed several hurried gulps before he swung his legs over the side of the bed.

"I really shouldn't take time to eat, Isabelle. If I don't get home, I—my family is going to send the law out looking for me."

Her brows shot up. "Really? Aren't they used to you being out all night?"

His face hot, he purposely set the coffee aside and reached for his clothing. "Not like this. Not overnight."

"Oh."

He pulled on his boxers and jeans before he glanced at her. She looked confused and skeptical, which made him even more frustrated with himself. Holt had always made special rules for himself regarding women. And he'd always followed them. Until now.

Standing, he zipped and buttoned his jeans. "That doesn't ring true with you, does it?"

"I didn't say that." She moved close enough to rest her hand on his forearm. "And frankly, it doesn't matter. That was then, this is now. Anyway, we agreed there'd be no strings. Remember?"

Hell, was she going to keep bringing that up? He was getting tired of hearing it.

That's the way it has to be, Holt. Keeping things casual is the best way for both of you. She won't get hurt when your eye starts to stray elsewhere. And you won't give it a second thought when she finds herself another man.

The mocking voice in his ears made his head throb and he reached for the coffee cup. Caffeine was all he needed right now, he assured himself. That and a plate of food. The rest would fix itself once he got home to Three Rivers.

After several more sips of the hot liquid, the bitter taste in his mouth eased enough for him to speak. "Yeah, I remember."

She studied his face for a long moment,

then stepped closer. "Holt, are you regretting last night?"

The confusion on her face suddenly wiped away the turmoil going on inside him. He placed the coffee back on the nightstand and wrapped his arms around her. "Oh, no, Isabelle. Last night was incredible."

She tilted her face upward until their gazes locked. "It was that way for me, too," she said softly.

Everything about her was warming him, touching him in ways that tilted his common sense and went straight to his heart.

You don't have a heart, Holt. You have lust and pride and a man's ego, but when it comes to women, you're lacking a heart.

Shoving aside the brittle voice in his head, he smiled and rested his forehead against hers. "You know, those eggs sound mighty good."

"What about your family calling out the law to search for you?" she teased.

He pressed a tiny kiss between her brows. "My family might as well get used to me being gone. 'Cause the two of us are just getting started."

Chapter Ten

February arrived with a wallop. Only this morning, Isabelle had spotted a few bits of snow flying on the north wind. After living in Albuquerque for two and half years, she'd gotten used to the cold winters and the heavy snowfall. But that didn't mean she liked it any more than Ollie and Sol did. Both men had shown up at feeding time dressed in heavy coveralls. Now, as Isabelle entered the cozy, warm interior of Conchita's coffee shop, she was grateful to be out of the bitter wind.

The clang of the cowbell over the door brought Emily-Ann up from behind the counter, where she'd been placing a tray of fresh pastries in the glass case. The moment she spotted Isabelle, her face creased into a smile.

"Well, I finally get a customer on this freezing morning and it happens to be one of my favorites," she said. "Hello, Isabelle. What are you doing out in this weather?"

Isabelle yanked off her mittens as she walked up to the glass counter. "A rancher's work never takes a holiday, even during bad weather. I had to come to town for a load of feed."

"I thought you had two ranch hands to do all that stuff for you."

"I still have them," Isabelle told her. "But I had a few more personal errands to run."

She pointed to a cake doughnut covered with white icing and chopped peanuts. "Give me one of those and a regular coffee with cream."

Emily-Ann looked surprised. "That's all? No apple fritter, or maple long john?"

Isabelle laughed. "Okay. Give me a cinnamon roll, too. The one with the raisins. That will be my attempt at a healthy diet today."

While Emily-Ann gathered her order, Isabelle walked over to one of the two small tables in the room and hung her puffy red coat on the back of one of the chairs.

"Good thing you're not busy," Isabelle commented as she took a seat. "I'd hate to have to eat outside in this weather."

Emily-Ann carried the coffee and pastries over to Isabelle and sat down across from her.

"I'm hoping this cold will blow out before Thursday. The Gold Rush Days celebration will be kicking off then."

Isabelle munched on the doughnut. "When I first drove into town, I noticed the banners crossing the street. Just what is this celebration?"

Emily-Ann's eyes sparkled. "Oh, it's

such fun. There's a carnival, plus all kinds of street vendors and entertainment. And then, of course, there's a big rodeo, too. This one will be the seventy-first annual celebration. It's been going on for a long time."

"Exactly what is being celebrated?" Isabelle asked.

Emily-Ann made a palms-up gesture. "I'm not much of a town historian, but it's to celebrate how the ranchers and miners first got the town going. Which was back in 1863—even a few years before the big city of Phoenix came into existence."

"That's interesting. So do very many people show up for Gold Rush Days?"

"Thousands and that is no exaggeration. It's always a busy time for everyone in town. Even with this street being off the beaten path, I get lots of extra customers. You should come join the fun. There's even a gold panning event. Who knows, you might get lucky and find a nugget." She cast Isabelle a clever look. "But from what I'm hearing, you've already found your nugget."

The doughnut in Isabelle's hand paused halfway to her mouth. "Me? I haven't been panning for gold. Even though Ollie and Sol tell me there might be some on my property. From what they say, one of the richest gold mines ever was somewhere in this area." She shrugged. "But I don't have time to chase after a fortune in yellow mineral. My dream is pastures filled with horses."

"Hmm. I thought since you started seeing Holt, your dreams might include a husband and children."

Isabelle stared at her. "Where did you hear that Holt and I were—seeing each other?"

Emily-Ann giggled. "Holt's sister Camille told me. We've been best friends since kindergarten. Her mother and sister keep her caught up on family happenings. Have you met all the Hollisters yet?"

Holt had been coming over to Blue Stallion Ranch to be with her almost every night, but so far he'd not invited her to Three Rivers or suggested she meet his family. Isabelle had been telling herself that none of that was important. The two of them hadn't been together for that long. They needed to focus on each other first before his family or her mother were involved.

Isabelle said, "The subject of meeting his family hasn't come up."

"Well, I figure it will. From what Camille says, the whole family believes he's besotted with you."

Isabelle made a scoffing noise. "Then they're overblowing the whole situation. Holt isn't falling for me. We're just— enjoying each other's company—for now."

Emily-Ann shook her head. "It's exciting to think of you and Holt together, but I'm kinda glad you're saying it's not serious with you two. Holt is gorgeous and sexy, but it would be heartbreaking to end up being just a notch on his belt. I'd rather have a simple man who loves me for real. Wouldn't you?"

Real love. That's what Isabelle wanted more than anything. And sometimes when she was in Holt's arms, when he was kissing her, touching her, she thought she felt love in the touch of his fingers, the taste of his lips. But she was afraid to believe or hope his feelings were the real thing.

"You couldn't have said it better." Isabelle reached across the table and patted her friend's hand. "What about you? Have you found anything close to that 'simple man'?"

"Me?" Her short laugh was scornful. "I've quit looking. There's something about me that turns men off. My red hair and freckles, I guess. Or I'm too big and gawky, or maybe I talk too much, I don't know. Anyway, most of the guys around here I've been acquainted with all my life. And they know about—"

Isabelle noted the somber expression on

her friend's face. "About what? Or would you rather not tell me?"

Emily-Ann's gaze dropped to the table-top. "It's hardly a secret. I'm from the wrong side of the track, I guess you'd say. My real father left town right after I was born. He never married my mother. She was from a poor background and his folks would've never stood for their son to marry a girl like my mom. Even though she was pretty and hardworking and honest—that wasn't enough. You know the kind."

Isabelle nodded. "Unfortunately those kind of snobbish people are very easy to find."

"Well, anyway, my grandparents kicked my mom out of the house. They never could forgive her for having a child out of wedlock. And just between you and me, I don't think they wanted to spend any money to help support us. But some-how Mom managed on her own to care for the both of us. Until she finally married a salesman who showed up one day in Wickenburg. He filled my mother's head with all sorts of big dreams. But he was nothing but a blowhard. None of the promises he made ever materialized. But the old saying about love being blind must be true. Mom believed every word he said. When she died, she was still waiting for the nice house and all the things that would've made her life easier."

"I'm sorry your mother is gone. And sorry that her dreams didn't come true," Isabelle said gently. "Does your stepfather still live here in Wickenburg?"

"No. Shortly after Mom died, he left and no one has seen or heard from him since. That's been ten or more years ago." She let out a long sigh. "So you see, I'm not exactly the sort of gal a guy takes home to meet Mama."

Isabelle grimaced. "That's ridiculous. You had nothing to do with your mother's decisions, or the way her family treated her."

"Isabelle, it's just like spilling something. The stain keeps spreading and spreading. That's how it is with me. The past spilled over and I can't outrun it or wash it off."

"Well, you shouldn't be trying to out-run or wash anything," Isabelle gently scolded. "And you know what I think? Some really nice guy is going to show up in your life and he's going to make you see just how special you are."

Emily-Ann's eyes grew misty as she gave Isabelle a grateful smile. "I'm so happy you came to live here, Isabelle."

"You know what, I'm pretty happy about it, too."

Blue Stallion Ranch was a beautiful piece of Arizona. The rugged hills and desert floors that made up the property were everything she'd been looking for. Given time and work and money, it would be thriving again. And the prospect was exciting.

But this past week and a half since she'd welcomed Holt into her bed, she'd come to realize that her dream of a horse ranch wasn't enough to give her complete happiness. Nothing would mean anything without him at her side.

She'd tried to gloss it all over with Emily-Ann and pretend that what she felt for Holt wasn't serious. But she couldn't delude herself. She was falling for the cowboy in the worst kind of way. Now she could only pray she wouldn't end up being just another name in his little black book.

When Holt unsaddled the two-year-old and started toward the ranch house, it was already dark. Any other time, he would've been feeling the fatigue of being in the saddle for the past five hours, but this evening he actually had a spring in his step. He was going to see Isabelle. He was going to talk to her and listen to her talk to him. He was going to eat with her, sleep with her, and make slow, delicious love with her. In short, being with

Isabelle was like stepping into paradise. Just the thought was enough to push the tiredness from his body.

As soon as he entered the back of the house and let himself into the kitchen, he knew something out of the ordinary was going on. The room was full of women-folk scurrying from one task to the next, including his sister Vivian.

She was standing at the cabinet counter, placing tiny appetizers on a silver tray. Wearing a vivid green dress that flowed over her pregnant waistline, she looked like she was dressed for a party.

"Sis, what are you doing here?"

She looked up and, with a huge smile, walked straight into his arms. "Hello, my naughty little brother!" Considering the girth of her belly, she gave him the best bear hug she could manage. "I thought I was going to have to go drag you out of the saddle to get you up here to the house!"

He dropped a kiss on the top of her

red head. "If I'd known you were here, I would've shown up sooner. What's going on anyway? Is it someone's birthday?"

She laughed and not for the first time Holt thought how beautiful she looked now that she was carrying her and Sawyer's twins. Her face glowed and there was a shine in her eyes that mirrored her happiness.

"Have you been hiding under a rock? Gold Rush Days are starting Thursday and Mom always throws a little party beforehand."

Oh, Lord, none of that had entered his mind. "Uh—yeah. It—just slipped my mind." He glanced quickly around the room. "Is Sawyer here? And Savannah?"

"They wouldn't have missed it for anything. Onida came, too." She winked slyly. "I think she didn't want to miss the opportunity of seeing Sam. She thinks he's a real gentleman."

Sam was the crusty old cowboy who worked as foreman for Tessa and Joseph's ranch, the Bar X. So if Sam was here, that meant Tessa and Joseph and Little Joe were here, also. Everyone would expect Holt to join in on the fun. Especially his mother, he thought with a pang of guilt.

"I've never been able to figure out what that old man has, but whatever it is, the women seem to like it. I think he's an older version of Holt Hollister," Vivian added with a cunning laugh.

Holt grunted with amusement. "I always did want to be like Sam."

She tapped a forefinger against his unshaven chin. "There's only one Sam and only one you. Thank God."

Holt patted the front of her protruding belly. "How're my little nephews? Isn't it about time for them to show their faces?"

"Not yet. And the boys or girls are doing fine. Just because you guessed the gender of baby Evelyn correctly doesn't mean you'll get lucky this time."

"It's a pair of boys. They'll probably

look just like Sawyer and grow up to break dozens of hearts."

She laughed. "Possibly. But your son, whenever you finally have one, will be the real heartbreaker."

Holt noticed Vivian said when, not if, he had a son. Marriage had really messed with her mind, he thought.

"You're dreaming, sis."

Vivian was about to reply when Reeva practically yelled from across the room. "Holt! What are you doing in my kitchen with those dirty chaps and spurs on? I don't want horsehair flying all over my food! Get out of here!"

"Excuse me, sis, I've got to go charm the cook."

He sauntered over to where Reeva was taking a pan of crescent rolls from the oven. "Reeva, why do you want to be mean to a hardworking man like me? All I want is a little love."

"Ha! Just like you don't get enough of that already." The cook playfully swatted a hand against his arm, which caused a puff of dust to billow out from his shirt-sleeve. "Get out of here and see if you can find some soap and water. We'll be eating in twenty minutes."

"Can't eat," he told her. "I have a date tonight."

She was stabbing him with a stern look when Maureen walked up behind him.

"Holt, did I hear you say you have a date tonight?"

He turned from Reeva's reprimanding frown to his mother's unsmiling face.

"You heard right," he told her. "I do have a date with Isabelle. Sorry, Mom. I didn't know about the party."

She rolled her eyes. "I've been having a Gold Rush Days party since before you were born. Every year at this same time. Where the heck have you been living, Holt, besides the horse barn?"

Normally he would've laughed at Maureen's scolding sarcasm, but not tonight. He worked his butt off and then some for

Three Rivers and there were times, like this one, when he felt his mother took him for granted.

"In case you haven't noticed, Mom, someone has to keep the ranch's remuda going," he retorted.

"Holt! You don't have to be so snippy," Vivian chided as she came to stand at his side. "This party is important to her and so is your being here. That's all she's trying to say."

"I have a life outside of this ranch and this family! And it's important to me!" He reached to the back of his leg and started unhooking the latches on his chaps. "I'll go have a drink with the men and then I'll be leaving."

He started out of the kitchen with the three women staring after him. He was almost into the hallway, when his mother's hand came down on his arm.

"Holt, just a minute," she ordered.

He turned to her and for an instant, as he took in her troubled face, he wanted to grab her into a tight hug. He wanted to rest his face against her shoulder as he had as a boy, feel her comforting hand stroke the top of his head, and hear her say that everything was going to be all right. But those days of his childhood were over and though he hated to admit it, his life, and the whole Hollister family, were changing.

"Mom, I apologize. I didn't mean to sound so short."

"I'm sorry, too," she said ruefully. "Nothing I said came out right. That's been happening too much with me here lately."

He shook his head, while feeling guiltier by the minute. His mother had an enormous workload on her shoulders. She didn't need any of her sons adding to her stress.

"I wasn't exactly Mr. Charming either," he admitted. "Look, Mom, if you want me to hang around for the party that badly, I can call Isabelle and cancel our date for tonight."

"No! That isn't what I want at all. You deserve time for yourself. I only—" She grimaced as she seemed to search for the right words. "You've been seeing Isabelle for a while now. I wish that you cared enough to have her over here to Three Rivers."

Did he care about Isabelle? Yes, he could admit that he cared for her. A lot. But he couldn't go so far as to say he loved her. No. That was for men like Blake and Chandler and Joseph. Not him. His mother should know that.

"I'll have her over," he promised. "Sometime. Whenever it's right."

Maureen knew he was hedging. Just like Holt knew it. But thankfully, she wasn't going to hound him about it tonight.

"I'll look forward to that day, son." She motioned on down the hallway to where his bedroom was located. "You go on and clean up. I'll tell Jazelle to make you a bourbon and cola. The good stuff that Sam gets," she added with a wink.

"Thanks, Mom."

She patted his check, then turned and headed back to the kitchen. Holt trotted on to his bedroom and after texting Isabelle a quick message to let her know he'd be running late, he jumped into the shower.

Short minutes later, he was buttoning his shirt when a light knock sounded on the door. Figuring it was Jazelle with his drink, he went over and opened it. But instead of Jazelle, it was Vivian.

"Here's your bourbon." She handed him a short tumbler. "Everyone else is going in for dinner. May I come in?"

"Sure. I'm just about finished here anyway." He tucked the tails of his shirt into his jeans, then walked over to the dresser and picked up a hairbrush. "But you should go on to dinner. You don't want to be late to join the others."

"It's okay. Sawyer is going to fill my plate for me. Double everything. To feed two babies. Or so he says. I think he just wants me plump." She eased onto the edge of his bed and looked at him. "I wanted to talk to you for a minute. We don't get to do much of that since I moved to the reservation. I miss you."

His throat tightened. Even though she was his sister, Vivian had been his best buddy since he was old enough to have a memory. Through good and bad, they'd stuck together. And even now, with her living some ninety miles away, he didn't have to wonder if she still loved him, or if she'd run to his side if he needed her. She'd be there in a heartbeat.

"I miss you, too, sissy. But you're happy with Sawyer and that's what counts."

"Happiness, I want that for you, too, Holt."

He cast a droll look at her. "Listen, I apologized to Mom for that outburst in the kitchen. And she apologized to me. We grate on each other's nerves sometimes. That's all. See, I'm so happy I can hardly stand myself."

She left her seat on the mattress and

came to stand in front of him. "Right now, I'm finding it very hard to stand you myself."

Seeing that she really meant it, he was taken aback. "What is that supposed to mean? You just said you missed me."

"I do miss you. In more ways than one. Because of the miles between us, yes. But I miss the old Holt, the adorable Holt, the one who wasn't trying to hide his feelings."

He tossed the hairbrush back onto the dresser top. "Carrying twins is affecting your eyesight, sis. I'm not trying to hide anything." Except that their father might've been an adulterer. And he was getting far more attached to Isabelle than he'd ever planned to be.

"Liar, liar, pants on fire. You know better than to try to fool me, Holt. You're getting in deep with this Isabelle, aren't you?"

He rubbed a hand against his forehead, then glanced at his watch. "As much as I love spending time with you, sis, I've got to run."

She threw up her hands. "Okay. Go ahead and run off. You just answered my question anyway. You've fallen for Isabelle Townsend."

"And what if I have?" He tossed the question at her. "What's the problem? You and everybody else in this family has always wanted me to find *the* woman."

"I'll tell you the problem. If you can't even admit to me that your feelings are serious, then how do you expect things to work with her?"

Holt grabbed his jacket from the closet and shouldered it on. "I don't expect it to work forever. Not like you and Sawyer will. I'm not built that way. But I love you for caring about me." He kissed her forehead. "Now go join everybody for dinner. And I'll talk to you soon."

Over on Blue Stallion Ranch, Isabelle glanced at the small clock on the end table. Nearly two hours ago, she'd gotten Holt's text explaining he'd be a little late. Just how late did he consider a little? At this rate, they'd be eating supper at midnight.

That first day Isabelle had walked up on Holt in the horse barn, she'd been struck by his rugged good looks, but she'd not missed the fact that he'd looked like he'd been running on empty for too many miles. After that initial meeting, she'd quickly learned that in a day's time he usually accomplished the work of two men.

Only yesterday he'd told her that the bulk of his mares had already foaled, so he'd been spending his time in the training pen, breaking two-year-old colts. It was a slow, painstaking job, along with being extremely dangerous. Holt's text message earlier this evening hadn't explained why he would be late. Now as time ticked on, without him showing up, she was beginning to worry that something had happened with one of his horses or, God forbid, to him.

The fire in the fireplace had turned to little more than a pile of burning coals, so she got up from the couch to add another log. She was finishing the chore when a sweep of headlights passed in front of the living room windows.

Relieved, she put away the poker and hurried out to meet him. As soon as he stepped down from the truck, she hugged him tight.

"I was beginning to think you weren't going to show," she said.

He kissed her cheek. "You got my text, didn't you?"

"Yes, but it's getting so late I was afraid there might've been some sort of accident."

"No. Just lots of company at the house." He wrapped his arm around the back of her shoulders. "Let's go in and I'll tell you about it. Got anything to eat?"

"Peanut butter and jelly sandwiches,"

she said, loving the warmth of his arm around her. "The pork chops and scalloped potatoes are ruined. Oh, but if you don't want the peanut butter and jelly, you can have bologna. I know you like that."

"Are you serious?"

The deflated look on his face had her laughing. "Yes. I'm kidding. I have the chops and everything to go with them in the warmer."

He playfully pinched the end of her nose. "You little teaser. I'm going to get you for that."

She let out a sultry laugh. "I'll just bet you will."

They entered the house and the first thing he noticed was the fire. "Wow, you built a fire for me? I feel special."

"That was my intention," she said, then tugged his head down so that she could kiss his lips.

"Mmm. You keep that up and those chops will have to stay in the warmer a little longer," he murmured, then kissed her twice more before she grabbed both his hands and tugged him into the kitchen.

"We'd better eat," she said. "You look famished and I'm starving. Let's fill our plates off the stove and carry them to the dining room. It'll be quicker."

"Sounds good to me."

Minutes later, they were eating at the long table, where Isabelle had lit a pair of candles and poured blackberry wine. Beyond the row of arched windows in front of them, the starlit sky shone down on the quiet ranch yard. The view was always beautiful to Isabelle but having Holt sitting across from her made it perfect.

As their conversation naturally turned to work, he asked, "How's the fence building coming along?"

"Good. We're making progress. And since we've moved farther away from the ranch yard, I'm finding more good grazing land. There's one little valley where Mr. Landry used to grow hay. I'm thinking I might like to try my hand at that.

Ollie and Sol seemed to know a bit about it. And they believe they can get the irrigation system going again."

He said, "Sounds like you've turned Ollie and Sol into big dreamers, too."

She pulled a face at him. "Ollie and Sol believe in themselves and me. The three of us plan to get all sorts of things accomplished—together. And to grow my own hay would be a big savings. Especially when my herd gets a lot larger."

He smiled. "You really love this place, don't you?"

"I do love it. Very much. It makes me feel—well, like I'm home. Really home. Do you understand what I mean?" she asked, then shook her head. "That's a stupid question. Of course, you understand. Three Rivers is undoubtedly in your blood the way Blue Stallion is in mine."

His fork hovered above his plate, while his green eyes made a slow survey of her face. "Is there anything that could make you move away from here?"

The question surprised her. Not only because he'd asked it, but because it was so easy to answer.

"No. I'm here to stay. Like I told you before, my parents were free spirits. While they were together, we moved around. Mostly to follow Dad's gigs, but sometimes just because my parents wanted something different. As a kid, I didn't know what it was like to put down roots. Later, Mom and I settled in San Diego, but city life wasn't for me. Then I thought I'd found a home in Albuquerque with Trevor. But that place was never really where I was meant to be." She gestured toward the window. "This is my land, my home. It's where I want my children to be raised. Where I want to live out my life."

"I figured that's what you'd say."

She wasn't going to ask him to explain what had prompted his question. She didn't know why, but she had the uneasy feeling she might not like his answer.

Picking up her fork, she began to tackle

the mound of scalloped potatoes on her plate. "You haven't told me about the company at Three Rivers tonight."

"Every year my mother throws a little family party in honor of Gold Rush Days. My whole family was there. Plus Matthew, our foreman, and Sam, the Bar X foreman. I think they were all a little peeved at me because I didn't stay."

A family party. Isabelle supposed she should feel honored that Holt had chosen to spend the evening with her. And yet, a part of her felt dejected because he'd not invited her to attend the party. With everyone there, it would have been the perfect time for him to introduce his new girlfriend.

But Holt might not think of her as his girlfriend, Isabelle pondered. In his eyes, she might just be a woman he had sex with and that's all she'd ever be.

Stop it, Isabelle! Quit feeling wronged or sorry for yourself! You went into this thing with Holt knowing who he was and what he was. You even told him there'd be no strings, so don't go thinking he's going to change.

Shutting out the taunting voice, she said, "I'm sorry you're missing the party, Holt. You should've told me. I wouldn't have been annoyed if you'd canceled your time with me."

The frown on his face slowly turned into a wan smile. "That's nice of you, Isabelle. But to be honest, I didn't want to stay for the party. I wanted to be here with you."

His words wrapped around her heart and she reached across the table and folded her fingers over his. "I'm happy you are here with me."

"So am I."

Chapter Eleven

In the past, Holt had never been bothered very much by his conscious. The only time he'd ever regretted his behavior was when he'd believed he'd disappointed his father or mother. Other than that, he was usually the to-hell-with-it sort. He tried to be a decent person, but he wasn't going to break his back trying to please everyone. If he offended or disappointed someone, it was their problem to get over it. Not his.

But tonight as he sat across the table from Isabelle, he suddenly realized he was a bastard. He didn't deserve her, or her sweet, understanding nature. If he had any decency about him at all, he'd put an end to this thing between them. He'd step away and let her find a good man, one who'd love her with all his heart.

Yeah, if he was a decent man, he could do that. But he was selfish and for most of his adult life he'd taken what he wanted and not worried about the consequences. And he wanted Isabelle. Wanted her more than he'd ever wanted anything in his life.

"Are you going to attend any of the Gold Rush Days celebration in town?"

Her question broke into his troubled thoughts and he looked over to see she'd finished the food on her plate.

"I used to go to the rodeo," he said. "But not these days. I have too much work at the ranch."

"I do, too. But it sounds like fun. Emily-Ann tells me Valentine Street is filled with a carnival and all sorts of interesting vendors. She thinks I should try my hand at gold panning." She paused and laughed. "I told her I could do that right here on the ranch."

He swallowed the last bite on his plate and pushed it aside. "You might find a nugget or two. The ranch hands on Three Rivers sometimes find rocks with streaks of gold. And Blake and Joe found a couple of nuggets in the same gulch where they believe, uh, where they found the scraps of Dad's shirt."

A thoughtful look suddenly came over her face. "Holt, did you ever think someone might have been digging around on your property for gold? I know it sounds far-fetched, but think about it. With gold prices what they are nowadays, one nugget would be worth a lot of money. Your father could've run across a trespasser and a fight ensued."

"That's a very logical deduction. But that's not what happened," he said resolutely.

Her brows arched. "How can you say

that? You told me that you don't know what actually happened concerning your father's death."

Unable to look her in the eye, he rose to his feet and gathered up his glass and plate. "Trust me. It didn't happen that way!"

He carried his dirty dishes to the kitchen with Isabelle following directly behind him.

As she began to put the leftover food in plastic containers, she said, "I'm sorry I theorized about your father's death, Holt. I realize it's not something you want to talk about."

Holt watched her place the containers in the refrigerator and walk over to the coffee machine. He should've already told her that she looked extra beautiful tonight in a long, blue and green skirt that swished around the tops of her cowboy boots and a matching green sweater tucked in at her tiny waist. It amazed him how she could go from a rough and tumble ranching woman to a soft, feminine siren. But then everything about Isabelle amazed him. That was the problem.

"Would you like coffee and dessert? I have ice cream. Or candy bars. The kind with caramel and nuts."

He walked over to where she stood and wrapped his arms around her. The feel of her soft body next to his was like a sweet balm that filled him with goodness. "I don't want anything—except to hold you. Make love to you."

She tilted her face up to his and he kissed her for long moments before he bent and picked her up in his arms.

With her hands locked at the back of his neck, he carried her to the bedroom and carefully placed her in the middle of the mattress. Then without bothering to remove his clothing or hers, he lay down beside her and gathered her into his arms.

His lips hovering near hers, he said, "I think about you all day. About you.

About being inside you. You're making me crazy, Isabelle."

She slipped her arm around his neck. "That's the way it's supposed to be. Crazy good."

With a groan that came from deep within him, he completed the connection of their lips and kissed her deeply, urgently. Her desperate response caused desire to erupt in him, arousing him to an unbearable ache.

Mindlessly, he rolled her onto her back and pushed the hem of her skirt up to her waist. She moaned as he hooked his thumbs beneath her lace panties and peeled the scrap of fabric down around her ankles and over her boots.

The urge to be inside her was pounding in his brain, gripping every cell in his body. There could be no holding back. No waiting.

His hands shaking, he managed to unzip his jeans and release his arousal, but that was as far as he got before she grabbed his hips and pulled him into her.

The hot, frantic connection wiped all thought from his brain, except that Isabelle was beneath him. Her arms were around him and her lips and breaths were merged with his. His thrusts were rapid and each time she rose up to meet him, she took more and more of him. And each time he felt his control slipping.

He was going to die right here in her arms. And he was going to die a happy man. The fateful thought was flashing through his mind just as she cried out.

"Oooh—Holt! Hold me—hold me tight!"

He tried to answer her pleas, but his body wouldn't cooperate. In the next instant he felt everything pouring into her until there was nothing left of him, except a beating heart. And even it wanted to belong to her.

When Holt eventually returned to earth, he felt as if he'd been on a long, long journey and his body was too spent to take another step. As to what had just occurred between them, he couldn't define it, much less understand why this woman made him lose all control. But he did realize one thing: the whole thing scared him more than anything he'd ever encountered.

He rolled away from her and with a forearm resting against his forehead, fought to regain his breath.

Next to him, Isabelle stirred, then draped her upper body over his.

"That was pretty darned incredible, cowboy," she whispered against his cheek. "Just think how good we might be if we ever get our clothes off."

He chuckled, then silently groaned, as her lips came down on his and the fire in his loins started all over again.

Three days later, on Friday night, Isabelle had been expecting Holt to show up for supper and she'd taken the time out

of her busy day to put a roast and vegetables in the oven. But shortly after dark
he'd called to inform her that one of his
young mares was about to foal and he
didn't want to leave Chandler with the
job of watching over her.

She'd understood his dilemma, but for
the past three nights, he'd called with a
reason he couldn't see her. True, they'd all
been legitimate reasons. But she was getting the impression there was something
else going on with Holt.

Was he getting ready to end things with
her? He'd not said anything that hinted
at those types of feelings. But then he'd
definitely not spoken about how much he
needed or loved her. No. Holt would probably never say the *L* word to her. Because,
whatever he was, he wasn't a liar. He'd
be blunt and painfully honest before he'd
lead her on with words he didn't mean.

Oh, well, she thought, as she bit back
her disappointment. Tomorrow was another day. And the food wouldn't go to

waste. Ollie and Sol would be more than happy to eat it.

With that thought in mind, she donned a coat, placed the roast pan into a cardboard box, and carried it out to the barn.

The door to Ollie and Sol's bunkroom was closed to shut out the cold night air. Isabelle stepped up on the wooden step and started to knock when she caught the sound of the men talking and one of them said her name.

She'd never been one to eavesdrop. A person rarely heard good things said behind his or her back.

With that old adage in mind, she raised her knuckles to the door, then let them drop a second time as Holt's name was spoken by Ollie.

"Have you noticed Holt hasn't been over here in the past few days?"

"Yep, I've noticed," Sol said. "I'd be blind not to."

"Yeah," Ollie said after a moment. "As

much as I like the guy, I hope he stays away."

There was a long pause and during the intermission, one of the female barn cats began to weave around Isabelle's legs and meow up at her. No doubt, the cat smelled the roast. Isabelle just hoped the men didn't hear her loud cries and open the door.

Finally, Sol said, "That's bad for you to talk that way about Holt. After all the man has done for us. Why, even now he's paying our way."

Paying their way? What did that mean?

She held her breath and refrained from placing her ear against the wooden panel. If one of them suddenly opened the door, she didn't know how she'd explain herself. She wouldn't be able to. She'd simply have to confess that she'd been listening in on their private conversation.

"That's all well and good," Ollie retorted. "But that doesn't mean we're blind to his ways. We both know if this keeps up, he's going to hurt Isabelle. And I don't mean just hurt her pride. He's gonna break her heart wide-open. I can see it coming."

There was another long stretch of silence and then Sol said, "Well, I'm thinking that she loves him, Ollie. We can't just come out and tell her she needs to stop seeing Holt. We're just a pair of old widowers. Neither one of us have had a wife in years. We don't know anything about the way young folks feel and think nowadays. Besides, she'd probably tell us it's none of our business."

"Don't guess it is," Ollie remarked. "But being her ranch hands sorta makes us her caretakers in a way. And I sure hate to see her heart broken. We both know Holt will never settle down with just one woman. And he'd sooner jump off a cliff before he'd get married."

"Yeah," Sol soberly agreed. "Isabelle's too good for that. She needs a man who'll marry her and help her run this place.

Holt is a Hollister through and through. He wouldn't leave Three Rivers for any reason. And sure not for a woman."

After a moment, Ollie said. "Let's talk about something else. Something happier. Are we going to the parade in the morning?"

"We haven't ridden in the Gold Rush Days parade in years. Why would we go now?"

"I don't know. Might be fun if we dug out our fancy chaps and spurs. We might catch the eye of some widow women."

"Hell." Sol snorted. "What would we do with widow women? Invite them out here for a cup of tea?"

"Well, what would be wrong with that? Isabelle drinks coffee with us. She likes it."

"Yeah, but Isabelle is different."

Isabelle had heard more than enough. She blinked back the foolish tears in her eyes and knocked on the door.

Sol opened the door and looked at her

with dismay. Hopefully he didn't have a clue she'd been standing on the step for the past five minutes.

"Hey, guys, would you two like some supper?"

"Why, Isabelle," he said. "What are you doing out in the cold and dark?"

She did her best to put on a cheery smile. "I cooked a roast and vegetables for Holt, but he can't come tonight. I thought you two might want to share it."

Ollie's face suddenly appeared over Sol's shoulder. "That's nice of you to think of us, Isabelle. And it sure smells good. You want to come in and eat with us?"

Handing the box to Sol, she said, "Thanks, but I've already eaten and I have some chores in the house to finish before bedtime. You two enjoy it." She started to leave, then on second thought turned back before the men had a chance to shut the door. "Uh, I forgot to mention it earlier this evening, but if you two would like the day off tomorrow to go to Gold Rush Days, it's okay with me."

Sol's solemn face brightened considerably. "Thanks, Isabelle. Are you going to go? Me and Ollie might get in the parade. You could watch us ride down the street."

Ollie elbowed him in the ribs. "Goofy, she sees us on horseback every day. She might want do something else. Like go to the carnival."

Any other time, Isabelle would be laughing at the two men. But tonight she could hardly keep her voice from wobbling. "No. I won't be going to town. I have something else to do," she told them. Something she should have done from the very first day she'd met Holt Hollister.

Back in the house, she sat down at the kitchen table and picked up her phone. Gabby had been ringing her earlier, but she'd been outside helping finish the evening chores. After that, she'd gotten busy with supper, until she'd gotten Holt's inauspicious call.

Now, as she punched her mother's number, Isabelle wondered what she was going to tell her. What could she tell her? That she was happy? That everything was wonderful? Three days ago, she'd thought everything was great. In fact, the intensity with which Holt had made love to her had almost made her believe he was really beginning to care for her. Perhaps even falling in love with her.

But now her eyes were wide-open. And they were filled with stupid, useless tears.

"Hello, Issy! I gave up on you calling back. I was about to step into the shower."

"Sorry, Mom. Go ahead with your shower. I'll catch you later."

"No! I'm already wrapped up in my bathrobe and taken a comfy seat on the end of the bed. I just wanted to see how things are going and if you'd taken time to call your father."

Isabelle tried to swallow the lump

around her throat. Her mother had lived without a loving husband for more than twenty years and she was happy. Isabelle could be happy, too. Just as soon as she got Holt out of her system.

"I called Dad yesterday. He sounded good, but like he was on another planet, as usual. He's been working on some new arrangements," Isabelle explained. "You know how preoccupied he gets."

Gabby laughed knowingly. "Why do you think I'm living alone? Bless his heart, he can't help himself."

Just like Holt couldn't help his fascination for horses and women, she thought sadly. In the very plural sense.

"So how are you and your rancher friend getting on? Holt? Isn't that his name?"

"Forget his name, Mom." Isabelle's throat was so tight she could scarcely speak. "Because I'm definitely going to forget him!"

Gabby went silent for a long stretch. Then she said, "Okay. What's wrong?"

Isabelle explained how she and Holt had been seeing each other on a regular basis until the past three days. Then she went on to relate everything she'd overhead Ollie and Sol discussing.

"Oh, Issy, you're being unreasonable and unfair. You can't make that sort of snap judgment just because your ranch hands think Holt is the wrong man for you. That's crazy thinking!"

"Yes, it would be. But Ollie and Sol know Holt just as well as anyone. They've worked around him for years."

"Yes, but people change, darling. Now that Holt has been dating you, he might be thinking differently."

"When I first mentioned Holt you didn't approve of me seeing another wealthy man, Remember?" Isabelle asked pointedly.

"That's because I spoke before I thought," Gabby said. "Having money or several girlfriends in his past doesn't make him a bad person. Nor does it mean he's the wrong man for you."

Her mother had always had a Polly-anna sort of view on everyone and everything. Isabelle sometimes wished she could be more like Gabby. But where Holt was concerned, she had too much of a realistic streak in her to believe he was a changed man.

"Oh, Mom," she said in a choked voice. "This misery is all self-inflicted. I knew all about Holt before I ever agreed to date him. I kept warning myself, but I couldn't resist him. And now I have to own up to the fact that I've made another mistake with a man."

"You've fallen in love with him, haven't you? I can hear it in your voice. I can hear the tears. Oh, Issy, I think—well, I can step away from the art exhibit for a weekend. I'm going to catch a flight up there!"

"No! No! And no! You've been waiting years for a break like this. You're not going to mess up the exhibit because of me. I'll be fine, Mom. Really."

Gabby was slow about replying and when she finally did, Isabelle was relieved that she sounded reassured.

"All right, honey, if that's the way you want it."

"I do. Now I need to get off the phone. I have laundry to do."

She told her mother goodbye, then hung up and promptly burst into tears.

Early the next morning, Holt was sitting at his desk, trying to sift through a list of hay suppliers, but Isabelle's voice kept drifting through his mind and getting in the way.

To grow my own hay would be a big savings. Especially when my herd gets a lot larger.

She was always so animated when she talked about Blue Stallion. She loved the land and the horses with equal passion. But what about Holt? In lots of ways, she'd showed him that she cared about him. But she'd never said the word *love* to him, or even hinted that she might be falling in love with him.

But you've felt it in her kiss, Holt. You've felt it every time she puts her arms around you. Each time she welcomes you into her bed. That's why you've been finding excuse after excuse to avoid seeing her. You're afraid that you're falling for her, too. And you don't know how to stop it. Other than stop seeing her completely.

To hell with that, he silently shouted back at the arguing voice in his head. He wasn't going to stop seeing Isabelle. She was the only thing that made his life seem worthwhile.

Shaking his head, he tried to refocus his attention on the list in front of him. Burl Iverson, Kern County, California; Walter Williamson, Churchill County, Nevada; Renaldo Ruis, Fresno County, California. The list continued, but Holt's attention was drawn away once again as he caught the sound of a woman's voice just outside the door.

Dear God, he was beginning to hear Isabelle's voice everywhere.

"Thank you, Matthew. You're very kind."

That was her voice! She hadn't said anything about coming here to see him. And at this early hour!

He jumped to his feet just as she was stepping through the open doorway. Her usual smile was nowhere to be seen. In fact, she looked drawn and peaked.

"Isabelle! What are you doing here?"

She carefully shut the door behind her, then walked over and took a seat in one of the chairs in front of his desk.

Not bothering with a greeting, she said, "Don't worry. I'm not here to ask you to introduce me to your family. I'll be gone before they ever know I'm here."

The bitter tone in her voice knocked him off-kilter for a moment. "I'm not sure what that is supposed to mean. But you meeting my family isn't worrying me."

"I'm sure it isn't. Why would it?"

"I don't know. Why would it?" he repeated inanely.

She crossed her legs and tapped the air with the toe of her cowboy boot. This morning she was wearing a pair the color of butterscotch. Tiny metal studs covered the tops and the slanted heels, and he didn't have to be told they cost a fortune. Clearly she wasn't here to walk through the horse paddock, he thought wryly.

"Why would you worry about something you never intended to do in the first place?" she asked, then shook her head. "Sorry, Holt, I'm going at this all wrong. I didn't come here this morning to be curt or tacky. I wanted to be nice about all this. That's the way two people who've shared the same bed should be to each other, wouldn't you say?"

"Nice. Naturally, I would." He walked around the desk and looked down at her. "I'm not yet sure what this visit is about, but I'm glad to see you."

She swallowed hard and as he watched her features tighten, he realized something was very off with her. This wasn't the Isabelle he knew, the Isabelle he'd spent hours with, the one who made him feel as if he was the only man in the world.

"Are you?" she countered.

"Look, Isabelle, if you're angry because I've not been over—" He broke off as she began to shake her head.

"I'm not angry," she said. "I understand you have more work on your shoulders than any one man should have."

Folding his arms across his chest, he said in a slow, inviting voice, "Okay, so if you're not angry, then why aren't you kissing me? Why aren't you telling me how much you've missed seeing me?"

Her sigh was weary. "Because I'm not going to kiss you anymore. I'm not going to see you anymore. Period."

Her words were like a punch in the jaw and he reached backward to clamp a steadying hand around the edge of the desk. "Isabelle, I'm well aware that you like to tease, but this isn't amusing. Frankly, I don't like it."

Her head dropped and Holt was faced with the shiny crown of her blond hair. The other night when she'd talked about finding gold nuggets, he could have told her he'd found his treasure when she'd come into his life. But he'd kept the thought to himself. He didn't dare utter anything she might take to heart. That was the way a man like him had to be.

"I'm not teasing, Holt. Whatever we had between us is over."

"Who says? You? Isn't that a one-sided decision?"

She looked up at him and Holt was shaken by the emptiness he saw in her blue eyes.

"Probably," she answered. "But I'm sure you've made more than your share of those one-sided decisions before. You understand the drill."

He frowned with confusion. "I'll tell

you one thing I don't understand—this—you! Do you think I've been seeing another woman? Is that what this is about?"

"I don't think you're seeing other women. Not now, but you will soon." Shaking her head, she stood up and stepped close enough to place her hand on his arm. "Holt, it's become clear to me that the two of us are headed nowhere. At first I told myself that didn't matter. But I can't keep fooling myself. It does matter. All those evenings I waited and watched for you to come to Blue Stallion, I asked myself why I was devoting so much time and emotion. Just to have you in my bed? That's not enough, Holt. And it's my fault for ever thinking it could be."

The anger that poured through him was far more potent than a double shot of Sam's bourbon. He wanted to ram his fist into the wall. At least he could think about the pain in his hand, instead of the one that was boring a hole in the middle of his chest.

"Oh, this is perfect, Isabelle. This coming from a woman who insisted she didn't want strings between us. Now you're whining because there are no strings."

Her nostrils flared as two red spots appeared on her cheeks. Dear God, she was so beautiful, he thought, so perfect. What was he doing? Had he lost his mind?

No. He was hanging by his fingernails, he thought. He was desperately trying to hold on to his life the way he'd always lived it. The only way he could live it. Without fences or restraints.

"I'm not whining, Holt. I'm walking out. Because I can see the future that I'm dreaming of is nothing like the one in your mind."

He sneered. "Oh, that's right. I keep forgetting you were born to a couple of dreamers. And you have to be just like them—always carrying around a fantasy. What is it now? Rainbows and unicorns? A fairy tale where some prince appears and makes everything perfect for you?

Well, I don't want a dreamer. I want a real flesh-and-blood woman!"

Her teeth snapped together. "Good! Because I don't want a man like you! You're just like Trevor—incapable of giving your heart—your love. And as far as I'm concerned, you can go find yourself a real flesh-and-blood woman. Gold Rush Days has Wickenburg brimming over with people. Today would be the perfect time for you to start looking for one!"

She turned to walk away and he instinctively reached out and caught her forearm. "You're wrong, Isabelle."

Her blue eyes darkened with shadows. "I only wish I were," she said soberly, then quickly added, "Don't worry about your brown mares. I'll have Ollie and Sol bring them to you."

The brown mares. The mares he'd wanted for her and only her. He felt sick to his stomach.

"I don't want the mares! Keep them!"

She pulled her arm from his grasp. "I

don't want anything that doesn't belong to me."

There was nothing for him to do now but to watch her walk out the door. But even after she was gone, her soft scent lingered about him, her cutting words continued to wound him.

Holt was still standing in the same spot, trying to compose his fractured emotions, when Blake knocked on the door frame and stepped into the room.

"Was that Isabelle I just saw driving off?"

Holt shoved out a heavy breath and managed to walk around to the back of the desk. As he sank limply into the executive chair, he said, "Yeah. That was her."

Blake poured himself a cup of coffee and took a seat. "Why didn't she hang around? You know how much Mom has been wanting to meet her."

Avoiding the truth would be pointless now, Holt thought miserably. He cleared his throat, but his voice still sounded like he'd been eating chicken scratch. "Mom might as well know that meeting Isabelle isn't going to happen. She just dumped me."

Blake's jaw dropped. "Is this one of your jokes?"

Holt was suddenly furious at himself and the waste of it all. He'd been stupid to attempt to have anything remotely close to a long-term relationship with a woman. Or to think he could ever have what his brothers had with their wives. "No! It isn't anything to joke about, Blake."

Over the rim of his coffee cup, Blake carefully studied Holt's mutinous face. "Well, well. A woman has finally dumped my little brother. How does it feel?" he asked, then barked out a short laugh. "Forget I asked. Whether you did the dumping or she did, you must be feeling damned relieved."

Holt wasn't relieved. He was angry and sick and crushed. Most of all, he was afraid. Scared to even think of the coming days without Isabelle.

Rising from the chair, Holt tugged on his jacket and plopped his hat onto his head. "As much as I appreciate this brotherly visit, I have things to do," he muttered.

Blake frowned at him. "Go ahead. Run off. But before you do, I'll tell you straight out, I'm glad Isabelle put an end to this."

Holt pierced him with a steely look. "Can you explain that?"

"Easily. You're not equipped to handle a woman like her. And I don't want to see you unhappy."

Blood was suddenly boiling beneath Holt's skull. "You do manage Three Rivers, Blake, but that doesn't mean you manage my life," he practically shouted. "And while we're at it, I'll tell you something. If it turns out that our father was a cheating bastard, then our sisters are going to know about it! You and Chandler and Joe might think you know what's best for everybody else, but I have a say in this, too!"

"Holt! What—"

Holt didn't stay around to hear more. He stalked out of the office and didn't stop until he reached the mares' paddock. But even though he was a quarter mile away from Blake's know-it-all advice, he found no relief from the anger and pain inside him. The sight of the mares milling around in the small pasture only made it worse.

If Ollie and Sol showed up with the brown mares, he'd send the men right back to Blue Stallion Ranch with their load. The mares were a symbol of the day he'd spent with Isabelle in Tucson and the night they'd first made love. The horses were meant to be on Blue Stallion—with Isabelle.

And him? Well, he was going to get out his little black book and find a woman who'd make him forget.

* * *

Nearly two weeks later, on Friday evening, Holt was sitting in the den, having a drink with Chandler. A half hour from now, he needed to head to town, where he was meeting his tenth different date in as many nights. He wasn't looking forward to it. Hell, he'd rather pull out his back molars with a pair of fencing plyers than to go pretend he was having a good time. Pretending that the woman sitting across from him was piquing his interest mentally, or sexually.

So why are you doing this, Holt? Why do you keep going through this long list of ladies, when you know none of them are going to wipe Isabelle from your mind? She's burned into your brain and no matter what you do, she's going to remain there.

The mimicking voice in his head was like a propaganda message being shouted repeatedly over a megaphone. And if it didn't stop soon, he was going to go crazy, Holt thought.

"Well, look who's here! Our beautiful sister," Chandler said, suddenly breaking into Holt's miserable ponderings.

Holt looked around to see Vivian strolling into the den. Since she was still wearing her ranger uniform, it was obvious she'd driven straight here to Three Rivers from her job at Lake Pleasant. He couldn't imagine what she was doing here, but he was more than pleased to see her.

Rising to his feet, Holt said, "Hi, sis. This is a nice surprise."

Chandler rose, too, and both brothers kissed their sister's cheek.

"Did you forget and think you still lived here at Three Rivers?" Chandler teased.

Vivian chuckled. "No. Pregnancy hasn't confused the navigation system in my head. I do still remember east from west."

"Sit down and I'll make you something to drink," Holt told her. "Take the chair by the fire. It's cold out this evening."

"Just a bit of sparkling water or juice," she told him as she sank into the wing-back chair. "I can't stay long."

While Holt went to a small bar in the corner of the room to get the drink, Chandler's phone began to buzz.

"You two are going to have to excuse me," he said as he scanned the message. "Roslyn needs me upstairs. Evelyn is throwing one of her fits. The little diva never wants to get out of the bathtub."

"Tell me about it," Vivian said with a laugh. "I have a fourteen-year-old diva."

"Bah!" Holt said as he handed her a small glass of orange juice. "Hannah has never been spoiled. Well, there might've been a few occasions when I spoiled her a little."

"You certainly did—letting her ride those wild two-year-olds when I wasn't looking. It's a wonder she didn't break every bone in her body!"

He eased down in the matching chair across from her and took a long sip of his drink. It was the second one he'd had this evening, and since he'd not eaten anything but a few bites of gooseberry pie early this morning, his stomach was more than empty. Now the bourbon was going straight to his head. Thank God. He didn't want to have to think. Not about anything.

Vivian watched Chandler leave the room, then glanced over at Holt. She didn't appear to be in a happy mood, but he smiled at her anyway.

"That belly of yours is getting enormous," he told her. "Makes you look real pretty."

She eyed his half-full glass. "How much of that bourbon have you had this evening?"

"Not enough," he muttered.

She grimaced. "Aren't you wondering why I'm here?"

He shrugged. "I figured you came to see Mom. She's not made it in yet. She and Blake went up to check out some of the Prescott ranges."

She took a sip of the juice. "I know. She texted me."

"Oh." He darted a glance at her. "Then why are you here?"

"Because Mom and Chandler told me you looked like hell and I wanted to see if they were right."

His jaw tight, he stared into the fire. "Were they?"

"No. They were wrong. You look worse. What are you doing? Trying to commit a slow suicide?"

"I'm not trying to do anything," he lied. "I've just gone back to being good ole Holt. You know, the one that changes women as often as he changes wet saddle blankets."

"Don't try to play cool with me. I may not live in this house anymore, but I hear what goes on. And I hear you've been staying out late every night, dating one woman after another. Are you actually enjoying this marathon you're putting yourself through?"

He rose from the chair and stood on the hearth with his back to the fire. After swigging down a good portion of his drink, he said, "It's nice that you've always thought of yourself as my little mother, Viv. But in this case, I don't need your mothering. There's nothing wrong."

She snorted. "Don't try to give me any of your bologna. It won't work. And you might as well down the rest of that drink. Because you're going to need it after you hear what I have to say!"

He frowned at her. "I have a date tonight. In fact, I should be getting ready to leave right now. I don't have time for a lecture from my big sister."

"Cancel the date. You're not going anywhere."

The stern resolution on her pretty face got to him more than anything she'd said and he suddenly bent his head and closed his eyes against the onslaught of pain hitting his from every direction. Of the whole Hollister family, Vivian had always loved him the most. Just as Isabelle had loved him.

Oh, yes, he could admit that to himself now. Even if she hadn't so much as spoken the words to him, he'd known it and felt it in his heart. He'd just not wanted to acknowledge her feelings or think about what any of it meant to him. Now he could only wonder if he'd thrown away the most precious gift he could've ever been given.

Vivian's hand suddenly rested on his arm and he looked up to see she'd joined him on the hearth.

"Why did you let this breakup with Isabelle happen? And don't try to tell me your relationship with her was nothing. I can see how much you're hurting."

He groaned. "I didn't let it happen, Viv. She's the one who ended things."

"No. You did. Because you couldn't be honest with her. You couldn't tell her that you loved her or wanted to be with her for the rest of your life. No, that would have taken some guts. Courage that you don't seem to have."

He scowled at her. "What do you know about it?"

"Ha! You ask me that after all I've been through? Think about it, Holt. Before I met Sawyer, he was a known ladies' man. I didn't trust him any farther than I could throw him. Plus, he was just like you. He didn't believe he could ever be a husband or father."

Holt looked at her as he remembered back to those days when Vivian had been agonizing over falling in love with the wrong man, or so she'd believed. "I called you a 'fraidy cat back then," he recalled. "I told you that if you really loved Sawyer you needed to hold on to him and never let go."

She smiled. "That's right. Imagine me taking love advice from my tomcat brother. But I did. And because I did, I learned real love has a way of taking away all those doubts and fears we have.

If you let yourself grab hold of Isabelle and never let go, you'll learn that, too."

He scrubbed a hand over his haggard face. He had to find the guts to face Isabelle again, to tell her exactly how he felt about her. Otherwise, his life was going to be a big black hole. "She doesn't want me in her life. Not now."

"Since when would you let something like that stop you? Don't you think you can change her mind?"

"I don't know," he mumbled. "Maybe Holt Hollister has lost his mojo."

Laughing now, Vivian leaned over and kissed his cheek. "You'll never lose that, little brother."

The next morning, Isabelle tethered the brown mares beneath the tin overhang of the barn and began the chore of grooming them. Since there'd been a sprinkle of rain sometime during the night, the horses had enjoyed a roll in the damp dirt. Now dust flew as Isabelle moved the brush over the mare's back.

She'd never intended to keep the pair. She'd even loaded them in the trailer and had Ollie and Sol drive them over to Three Rivers Ranch. But they'd come back with the two mares and told her that Holt had refused to take them. After that, Isabelle had decided not to worry about the matter. If he wanted the mares, he knew where they were. He could send some of his hands to collect them.

"Need some help?"

Isabelle looked around to see Ollie walking up near the mare's hip. Sol was a step behind him.

"No. I got this." She continued to brush down the horse's shoulder. "It's Saturday. Aren't you guys going into town for coffee at the Broken Spur? There might be some single women hanging around just waiting to join you."

"We're going." Sol spoke up. "But we don't expect to see any women."

"Don't ever say never, Sol," Ollie told his buddy. "We might get lucky one of these days."

Isabelle glanced up just in time to see Sol frowning at Ollie and making a motion toward her. From the sheepish looks on their faces, she decided they wanted to discuss something with her but felt awkward about it.

"What's up, you two? Is there something you want to talk to me about? Are you needing a raise in salary?"

"Oh, no, Isabelle. We're making more than enough money," Sol was quick to answer.

"We don't need money," Ollie added. "You just forget about that, Isabelle."

She didn't see how the men could consider the meager amount of salary she paid them as plenty, but for now it was the best she could do. Later, when the ranch began to actually take in money, she'd do her best to give them a substantial raise. "Okay. Then what's on your mind?"

"We're wondering about Holt," Ollie answered. "He hasn't been here for a while. And when we hauled the mares over to Three Rivers, he wasn't exactly a happy camper. Did you two have a falling-out or something?"

Isabelle bit down on her bottom lip to stem the tears that burned her eyes. "Uh—I guess you could put it that way. I'm not seeing Holt anymore. I decided he—wasn't the right guy for me."

Sol exchanged a guarded look with Ollie. "We thought— To be honest, we didn't much think Holt was the right guy for you. But you were happy when he was coming around. You're not happy now."

It was all Isabelle could do to keep from bursting into tears. These past two weeks since she'd parted ways with Holt, she'd never hurt so badly or felt so empty inside.

"For a while there I was mixed up. I thought Holt was the right guy for me. But you two know Holt. He's not the marrying kind. And I want—well, I want more than just a boyfriend."

Ollie said, "Isabelle, if you're letting gossip about Holt sway your thinking, then you're messing up. Sure, he's been a bachelor for a long time, but he's a good man. Better than you probably even know."

Sol cleared his throat and frowned at Ollie. "It might take some doing, but me and Ollie figure if anybody can settle his roaming ways, it'd be you."

"That's right," Ollie added with a nod of his head. "If you care anything about him, you ought to go after him. You don't want some undeserving gal to snatch him up."

Isabelle pulled a tissue from the pocket on her jacket and dabbed her misty eyes. "Oh, guys, this doesn't have anything to do with gossip. I've been married once and that man didn't love me. I, uh, don't want to get into that again."

Ollie gave her a kindly smile while Sol patted her shoulder.

"We just want you to be happy," Ollie said.

"Yeah, that's what we want," Sol added. "So you think about what we said, Isabelle."

The two men must have decided they'd talked enough. Sol mumbled that they'd see her later and the two of them walked off. Moments later, she heard them climb into their truck and drive away.

Isabelle thoughtfully went back to grooming the mares, but all the while she brushed and curried, her mind was replaying everything she'd said to Holt and everything he'd said to her that last day she'd seen him at Three Rivers. The whole scene was like watching the world crumble around her.

He'd accused her of living with her head in the clouds, of fantasizing of a prince coming to make her life perfect. Was Holt right? Was she guilty of wanting too much from him? Expecting too much from the brief time they'd been together?

With Trevor, she'd waited for more than two years, hoping his feelings for her would turn into real love. It hadn't happened. She'd accused Holt of being just like her ex, incapable of giving his heart. But she'd flung those words at him out of hurt and frustration.

Holt wasn't like Trevor. He wasn't like any man she'd ever known. He was incredibly special. He was everything she'd ever wanted and she loved him. Now that she'd found him, she couldn't give up and let him slip away.

But would he be willing to try again? She wouldn't know the answer to that until she faced him and laid her heart out for him to see.

Determination fueling her, Isabelle quickly finished the grooming chore, then released the mares into a nearby paddock. As she hurried to the house, she decided not to text or call him. No. Better to catch him off guard, she thought, than to give him a chance to run from her.

Inside the house, she went straight to her bedroom closet and began searching through the hangered clothes for something suitable to wear. She needed something feminine. Something that would make her look irresistible to him.

No, she thought suddenly. She shut the closet door and walked over to the dresser mirror. The image staring back at her was a woman dressed for the job she loved. This Isabelle, in her jeans, yellow shirt, and dusty boots, was the essence of who she was and what she wanted. If Holt couldn't love her like this, then she truly needed to put him behind her once and for all.

With that decision made, she went back to the kitchen to collect her handbag and truck keys.

And then she heard it. The rattling sound of a stock trailer coming down the long driveway.

Who on earth could that be? Ollie and Sol hadn't taken a trailer with them. And it couldn't be a horse buyer. It would be a year or more before she began advertising Blue Stallion Ranch.

Deciding someone had taken the wrong backroad and was lost, she exited the front of the house and from the edge of the porch, peered out at the vehicle that was rolling to a gentle stop.

Oh! Oh, my! It was Holt's truck and an expensive-looking horse van hooked to it.

Her heart racing wildly, she watched him climb down from the cab and start toward the house. The moment he spotted her, he paused briefly, then continued striding toward her.

Fearful and hopeful at the same time, Isabelle stepped off the porch and began walking toward him, until the two of them met just inside the yard gate.

"Hello, Holt," she said, relieved that she'd managed to squeeze the words past her tight throat. "Are you here to collect your brown mares?"

The expression on his face was unlike anything she'd seen on him before. It was rueful and pleading and so raw that it made her ache just to look at him.

"Those aren't my mares," he said huskily. "Those are yours and ours—together. Remember? We're partners."

Tears filled her eyes and spilled onto her cheeks. "Are we?"

Groaning, he reached for her and Isabelle fell willingly into his arms. His face buried itself in the curve of her neck and she wrapped her arms tightly around him.

"Isabelle. My darling, Isabelle," he said hoarsely. "Will you forgive me for being a blind, stubborn fool?"

She let out a sob of joy. "I'm the one who should be asking for forgiveness. I'm the one who broke us apart. But only because—"

He eased his head back and looked deeply into her eyes. "We both know that everything you said that day in my office was true. That's why it made me so angry. For years, my family warned me that one day I'd find my match and fall in love. I didn't believe them. Until you forced me to see how empty my life would be without you. I love you, Isabelle. More than you can ever know."

Holt didn't just want her. He loved her! The knowledge caused something to burst inside her and send sweet, warm contentment flowing into her heart.

"Oh, Holt, I love you so much. But I was afraid to tell you. Afraid you didn't want to hear it."

"I didn't want to hear it," he admitted, "because it would've forced me to examine my own feelings." Smiling, he pressed his cheek against hers. "But I want to hear it now, Isabelle. Every day. For the rest of our lives."

She was trying to take in the wonder of those words when, a few feet behind them, a loud whinny sounded from inside the horse trailer. Across the way, the freshly groomed brown mares answered the call.

Isabelle eased out of his arms and looked at the horse van. The side windows were closed, blocking any view of the interior, but the subtle rocking movements told her a horse was inside.

Her gaze slipped back to Holt. "You brought a horse with you?"

Grinning, he caught her by the hand and led her out to the truck and trailer. "Not just any horse," he said, then with a hand on her arm, carefully guided her to a safe spot. "Let me show you."

A minute later, Isabelle stared in stunned disbelief as he backed the blue roan stallion down the loading ramp and onto the ground. "That's Blue Midnight! What is he doing here?"

His expression full of love and tenderness, Holt handed the horse's lead rope over to Isabelle. "He's yours now. He's going to make Blue Stallion Ranch more than just your dream, Isabelle. He's going to help turn this place into a prosperous horse farm for you—for us. That is, if you want me here with you."

"As my partner?" she asked.

"Your partner, lover, husband, and father of your children. Anything you want me to be," he told her, then with a big grin, added, "As long as I don't have to sleep in the bunkroom with Ollie and Sol."

"You want us to be married? But what about those strings you never wanted? What about your job at Three Rivers?"

She barely got the question out when Blue Midnight nudged her in the back and propelled her right into Holt's loving arms.

His hands cupped her face. "You can throw a lariat on me if you want—just as long as we're together. As for my managing the horse division at Three Rivers, I can still do that and help you, too. My family has been telling me to hire more trainers to ease my workload. The time has come for me to follow their advice." He brought his lips next to hers. "I want Blue Stallion Ranch to be my home—our home. Together."

"Oh, Holt, I'm so glad you've come home to Blue Stallion Ranch."

He closed the tiny distance between their lips and as he gave her a kiss full of promises, Blue Midnight looked over at the brown mares and whinnied a promise of his own.

Epilogue

"You know, roses are delicate and romantic. Most women like having a garden of roses in their backyard," Holt said as he peered down at Isabelle who was on her hands and knees, carefully planting a large barrel cactus. "But no, you want a garden of tough, thorny cacti."

Tilting her head back, she pulled a playful face at him. "That's right. How long do you think a rose would last in this blistering heat? Besides, cacti have beautiful blooms," she argued.

"They grow at glacier speed and you're lucky if they bloom once a year," he pointed out.

She stood up and brushed her gloved hands on the seat of her jeans. "You want instant gratification. That's your problem," she joked and poked a finger into his hard abs. "I honestly don't know how you bear to wait eleven months and twenty days for a foal to be born."

"Patience, my beautiful Isabelle. I'm brimming over with it. That's why I waited until I was thirty-three to find the perfect wife for me."

"Ha! You mean you waited until I chased you down. Or did you chase me?" She laughed and curled an arm around his lean waist. "It doesn't matter, does it? We caught each other."

A little more than six months ago, she and Holt had been married in a simple ceremony here on Blue Stallion Ranch. All of the Hollister family and a few of their close friends had attended, along with Isabelle's mother and father. Emily-Ann had acted as Isabelle's maid of honor, while Chandler had stood next to Holt as his best man.

Isabelle's dreams had come true that day as she and Holt had spoken their vows of love to each other. And since then, she could truthfully say she was happier than she could have ever imagined.

Holt nudged her toward the back door of the house. "The sun is going down. We'd better go in and get ready. If I know Reeva, she'll have Jazelle passing out drinks and appetizers two hours before dinner."

Tonight they were going to Three Rivers Ranch to attend Blake's fortieth birthday party. From past visits to the big ranch house, Isabelle knew there would be piles of delicious foods and all sorts of drinks, along with plenty of conversation and laughter.

"I'm going to miss seeing your mother tonight," Isabelle remarked. "Do you have any idea when she might be coming home?"

A little more than two weeks ago, Maureen had packed up and driven down to Red Bluff to visit her youngest daughter, Camille. Her decision to make the trip had been rather sudden and Isabelle knew the rest of the family didn't quite know what to make of Maureen's unexpected departure. All of them wondered if she'd gone down there with intentions of bringing Camille back to Three Rivers, or if she'd made the trip just as a way to escape whatever was gnawing at her.

"Blake heard from her last night. He said she sounded cheerful enough, but he couldn't pin her down as to when she might be coming home." He shook his head. "This isn't like her at all, Isabelle. Normally, she's content to be working around the branding fire or herding cattle."

"Well, you do you have a few cowboys working the ranch down there. Could be she's keeping busy helping them," Isabelle reasoned. "Or it could be that she simply wants to be with her daughter."

Holt nodded. "That's true. Camille has been gone for a couple of years now. I know Mom misses her." He wrapped an arm against her back and urged her into the house. "Come on, we can't let any of this dampen the party."

Inside the house, they walked through the kitchen and started down the long hallway to the bedroom. As they passed the open door to the guest bedroom, Holt said, "Speaking of mothers, where is yours? Isn't she going to the party with us?"

A month ago, Gabby had flown up from San Diego for an extended visit. So far, her mother had been having a blast getting to know the Hollisters and exploring Wickenburg and the surrounding areas. Isabelle loved having her mother's company and Holt seemed to enjoy her off-beat personality. Thankfully she made it a point not to intrude on their privacy.

"Yes. Mom's going to the party. But not from here. She's over at the Bar X with Sam. They'll be leaving for the party from there."

Holt paused to shoot her a comical look. "Gabby is with Sam?"

Isabelle laughed. "I know. It's hard to figure. She took one look at the old cowboy and flipped. Now she's talked him into sitting still long enough to let her paint his portrait."

Chuckling, Holt shook his head in amazement. "Do you really think she's attracted to him? In a romantic way?"

Isabelle made a palms-up gesture. "Who knows? I thought she was falling for the guy who exhibited her artwork. But she's obviously forgotten all about him."

They entered the bedroom and while Holt showered, Isabelle began to lay out the clothing she was planning to wear for the party.

"Isabelle? Are you sure you don't mind going tonight?" Holt called to her over the sound of the running shower. "I know it must feel like we go over to Three Rivers for some reason all the time."

She walked over to the open doorway of the bathroom to answer. "I love visiting with your family. Gives me a chance to see all the new babies. Vivian and Sawyer's twin boys, Jacob and Johnny, and Tessa and Joe's new daughter, Spring. And just think, it won't be long before Chandler and Roslyn have their second baby to go with little Evelyn. I think her due date is sometime before Halloween."

The shower turned off and Holt stepped out of the glass enclosure and wrapped a towel around his waist. The sight of his hard, muscled body never failed to excite her and just for a moment she considered stepping into the bathroom and pulling the towel away.

Grinning slyly, his wet hair tousled around his head, he walked over to her.

"Are you sure you don't have something to tell me? Like the smell of breakfast is making you sick?"

She tried not to smile. "Actually breakfast has been tasting better than ever."

"Damn."

Her smile grew coy. "Could be I'm eating for two."

His eyes grew wide. "Is that what I think it means?"

The eager hope in his voice told her how very much he wanted to be a father.

She nodded. "I made a doctor's appointment today. We'll find out for certain tomorrow."

"Oh, Isabelle, honey!" He pulled her into his arms and she laughed as she wrapped her arms around his wet torso. "This is fantastic! I'm going to be a father! Let's tell the family tonight. While everybody is there."

She leaned back far enough to look at him. "But, Holt, we don't know for certain yet."

He gently touched his fingertips to her cheek. "I'm certain. You have a glow in your eyes."

"That's because I'm looking at the man I love." She kissed him, then added slyly, "By the way, I thought you might want to know that Ollie and Sol made a confession today."

His brows arched. "That's good to hear. I'll bet the priest was exhausted before they ever finished."

She pinched his arm. "Not that kind of confession! They ratted on you. About how you paid them an extra salary long before we got married. Why did you do that?"

Pulling her close, he rested his cheek against hers. "Can't you guess? That was just my way of saying I love you, darling."

* * * * *

LET'S TALK
Romance

For exclusive extracts, competitions
and special offers, find us online:

f facebook.com/millsandboon

⊙ @millsandboonuk

🐦 @millsandboon

Or get in touch on 0844 844 1351*

For all the latest titles coming soon,
visit millsandboon.co.uk/nextmonth